"There's something in the trees. I'm going to investigate." Drawing his service weapon, Ryan flipped on his body camera.

"No!" Elise caught his hand. "What if you get hurt? Or worse?"

Warmth spread at the concern in her rich voice. "I have to go, Elise. We need to catch whoever is behind these attacks. You stay in the house. Lock the door behind me."

Despite the mutinous set to her mouth, he heard the bolt slide into place once he was outside. He started toward the trees. He had barely gone half the distance when his phone rang. It was Elise.

"Elise? What's wrong?"

"Ryan? Is that you outside?"

The tremble in her voice caught at him. Then he frowned; she'd watched him go outside.

"You know I am. I'm almost to the tree line. Are you okay?" The sense of foreboding spiked as he heard her take a harsh breath.

"I can see a shadow through the blinds... Someone is standing just on the other side of the window."

Dana R. Lynn grew up in Illinois. She met a man at a wedding who she told her parents was her future husband. Nineteen months later, they were married. Today they live in rural Pennsylvania with their three children, two dogs, one cat, one rabbit, one horse and six chickens. In addition to writing, she works as an educational interpreter for the deaf and is active in several ministries in her church.

Books by Dana R. Lynn

Love Inspired Suspense

Amish Country Justice

Plain Target
Plain Retribution
Amish Christmas Abduction
Amish Country Ambush

Presumed Guilty
Interrupted Lullaby

Visit the Author Profile page at Harlequin.com.

AMISH COUNTRY AMBUSH

DANA R. LYNN

HARLEQUIN® LOVE INSPIRED® SUSPENSE

Recycling programs
for this product may
not exist in your area.

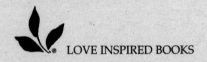

LOVE INSPIRED BOOKS

ISBN-13: 978-1-335-49054-4

Amish Country Ambush

www.Harlequin.com

Printed in U.S.A.

The Lord is my light and my salvation; whom shall I fear?
the Lord is the strength of my life;
of whom shall I be afraid?
—Psalms 27:1

To my editor, Elizabeth Mazer. I have been blessed by your incredible wisdom and guidance through the past few years. I appreciate you more than I can say.

ONE

The lights flickered as thunder boomed, rattling the windows. Immediately, heavy sheets of rain pelted the glass. Distracted, Elise St. Clair glanced at the lights running the length of the ceiling as she pressed the button to answer the next call.

Her customary greeting of "Nine-one-one. What's your emergency?" was swallowed up in the intensity of the noise that blasted back at her.

The woman on the other end of the phone was shouting, the sound deafeningly loud. And worse, she couldn't understand a word the woman was saying. She was yelling in Pennsylvania Dutch, the language spoken by the Amish community. Elise didn't quite recognize the voice, although there was something familiar about it. She glanced down at the screen nearest her and felt her world tilt.

She might not have recognized the voice on the other end of the phone, but she knew the address that flashed across one of the three computer monitors at her station.

It belonged to an old, slightly creaky farmhouse on the edge of town. The paint was peeling in places, and there were some shingles missing. It was hidden in the middle of nowhere. The kind of place people would drive by without a second glance.

It was also her house. The house she had lived in for the past two years with Mikey, her nephew who was now three years old. And the phone number belonged to her babysitter, Diana Mosher, who was definitely not the person on the phone. Where was Diana? Who was calling her?

Something horrible had happened, and she couldn't understand a word of it. The urge to throw down her headset and dash out the door was fierce. Her hands were already on the headset, ready to snatch it from her head before she realized that she was the only one who could notify the authorities of the need for help. But who should she call? Police? Ambulance? Fire department? As head dispatcher, it was her job to send the call to the correct department.

The shouting on the other end eased off as the woman on the line started sobbing. She sounded younger than Elise had first thought. Wait a minute. Her cleaning girl, Leah, was due in today. Elise had hired her because she herself was allergic to dust, and there was dust everywhere in a farmhouse in rural northwestern Pennsylvania. Leah was Amish. She spoke English and was able to communicate with Elise perfectly well—but if she was upset, and she definitely sounded upset, she might default to Pennsylvania Dutch.

"Leah?" A sob answered her. "Leah…it's Elise. What happened?"

"I think she's dead," Leah answered through her tears.

Diana? Fear and grief started to collide. *Not again. Please, God. Not again.*

Forcing a calm she didn't feel, Elise said, "Leah, what happened to Diana? Do you see Mikey? Is my nephew there?" She clamped her lips against the flood of hysteria threatening to break free.

On the other end, Leah sucked in a harsh breath. In the distance, Elise could make out a crash on the other end of the line. Not thunder—something else. Something more frightening. Then another crash. Something was happening.

"Leah? What's going on?"

Then a whisper. "I think someone's in the house."

The line went dead.

Elise froze for a second, gagging on the fear that closed her throat. She'd been too complacent. Tricked into a sense of false security. And now the danger she should have been expecting all along had found her again. Yes, it was possible that a complete stranger was breaking into her house, but she doubted it. Every instinct she possessed was shrieking that the attack was deliberate, and she was the intended target.

The memories she'd been running from swamped her. Her sister, Karalynne, murdered. Elise believed with all her heart that her overly possessive brother-in-law Hudson had killed Karalynne. But he'd disappeared. And she'd taken Mikey and moved away from the memories.

Could Hudson be responsible for this new attack?

She shook her head. The police had told her Hudson had died, a horrible violent death. She'd seen the report. Part of her had sighed in relief, choosing to believe she and her nephew were safe.

But now unease returned. As much as she wanted to believe Hudson was dead, there was one fact that had always bothered her. His body had never been found. The police had insisted that the car fire that had killed him had incinerated his remains. What if…

Enough! She had to get to Mikey. Because someone was after them. Although if it wasn't Hudson Langor, she didn't know who would have any reason to attack her home.

She should have warned Diana about Hudson. And about the brutal violence he was capable of. But without proof, who'd believe her?

If only she'd stayed home one more day! She'd had a nasty stomach bug that had kept her at home for the past two days, but today she'd felt well enough to come into work. Had she been home…

Elise couldn't worry about that. Not now. She had to get to Mikey. He was all that mattered.

Her coworker Monica Johnson sauntered into the room, a bored expression on her pretty face. She could do the job.

Elise whipped off her headset and jumped up so fast her wheeled chair was propelled back, slamming into the wall behind her. Monica stared at her, open-mouthed. Elise never got emotional at work. When handling frantic emergency calls, she felt that calmness on her end was key. But this wasn't a normal situation where she had to soothe a stranger into sharing the necessary details. This time, she was the one under attack, and she couldn't hide how frightened she was.

"Monica! Send the police to my address. Someone

broke in. And send an ambulance, too. My babysitter may have been injured. I'm heading there now."

Not Mikey. Please, God. Let Mikey and Leah be okay. Diana's image floated through her mind. *And if it's possible, please let Diana still be alive.*

Monica nodded, her face pale and shocked as she shooed Elise away. Elise could hear Monica's loud, abrasive voice as she called the police. Elise grabbed up her purse and flew out the door. Thankfully, it was only four o'clock in the afternoon. She wouldn't have to deal with traffic or darkness as she drove.

She hadn't counted on the rain, though, turning the muggy July day into a wet mess. Elise dashed to her car, her feet slogging through puddles as fat raindrops pounded relentlessly on her bare head. She hadn't thought to grab her umbrella on her way out the door, and she certainly wasn't going back for it now—not when every second counted.

She was soaked and shivering by the time she was seated behind the wheel. She started the engine and shifted into Drive. Clenching the wheel in both hands, she drove furiously, swerving to avoid the larger puddles. Even so, her right wheel hit one and water splashed up on the windshield.

Pulling onto her road, she spun the wheel and turned sharply into her long gravel driveway. Then she stopped. She couldn't see her house from here, but she could envision it clearly. The large farmhouse that had appeared so perfect to hide in when she'd first seen it now seemed like the perfect haven for a madman lying in wait to ambush her. If she drove all the way up the driveway, he'd hear the car and know she was coming. She had to walk. Decision made, she pulled the car off the driveway enough to let the emergency vehicles pass. Then she killed the engine. Her fingers fumbled on her seat belt. Finally, the buckle slipped free and she shoved it aside, her free hand scrambling for the door latch.

Leaving her purse in the car, she grabbed her keys and ran up the driveway. She was a good runner, but her anxiety had her breathing faster than normal. By the time she'd reached the side of her house, she was panting. Sweat, mixed with rainwater, dripped down her neck.

At the stairs, she paused. If she was going to assume the intruder was still inside, then she needed to consider her entrance carefully. If the attacker was Hudson, the man had a brutal streak that ran deep. While her heart urged her to get inside and find her nephew as quickly as possible, caution was advised, especially if she had any hope of saving Mikey and Leah. Where were the police?

Carefully, she pulled open the screen door. The heavy wooden front door was unlocked. It swung open with a faint creak. She cringed. Had Hudson heard that? She held her breath and listened. Nothing. The silence terrified her. Ten minutes ago, Leah had been shrieking. Now, aside from the still-pouring rain beating against the roof and windows, there was no sound at all.

She slipped in through the half-open door and glanced around. From this vantage point, she had a clear view of both the living room and the dining room. No one seemed to be there. She took a step into the open living room and approached the couch, which faced into the room. Something crunched under her foot. Glass. From where?

She lifted her eyes to look around and sucked in a shocked breath. Every single picture on the wall had been shattered, the familiar images damaged or destroyed. Her heart stuck in her throat. All she had left of her sister was wrapped up in pictures and her son. Now the pictures had been destroyed, and Mikey... Again, she shoved down the urge to run to his room. If she was going to protect him, she needed to be cautious— to carefully assess the situation rather than rush in. She continued her survey of the room.

Glass covered the hardwood floor. She could see shards sticking out of the oval area rug. A baseball bat was leaning against the wall. Behind the coffee table situated in front of the sofa, an arm was stretched out, the hand tapering into three perfectly manicured fuchsia-tipped nails. The other two had broken off. Diana. Averting her gaze, she reached out for the bat. There was something on it. Blood. She hesitated before her hands touched the bat, knowing it had been used as a weapon against her friend. The police would want it as evidence, so she should leave it alone—but on the other hand, it was a weapon she could use to defend herself. Torn, she left it alone for now.

Clutching her throat, she fought against the nausea that rolled in her belly and stepped farther into the room. Maybe Leah was hiding with Mikey deeper inside the house.

Glass crunched behind her.

"Well, well, well. Little Elise." She knew that voice!

Elise whirled, her heart in her throat as, for the first time in two years, she faced the one man she'd feared above all others. The handsome face she remembered was gone. The face before her was damaged, ravaged by fire to the point that it was no longer recognizable. The thick hair she'd seen him smooth back so often was thin, missing in places. Patches of scar tissue replaced hair in several places. The charming smile she remembered was now distorted due to the damaged skin and muscle tissue. It would have been tempting to believe she was facing a total stranger.

Except for the voice.

That voice she'd know anywhere. Dark and gravelly, cold and cruel.

"Hudson!" she gasped. "You're supposed to be dead."

He smiled. It was a smile filled with malice. Images of him strangling Karalynne flooded her mind, paralyzing her.

"You'd like that, wouldn't you? I'm sure it was you who convinced my wife to throw me out of the house. Which means you're to blame for everything."

He stepped closer. Dizziness swamped her. She wanted to run. But where was Mikey? Hudson reached out a large hand and grabbed a handful of her short curls. Pain lanced through her skull as he pulled her head back. She cried out. "Not so brave now, are you? You should never have interfered in what didn't concern you. You turned her against me, I'm sure you did. She never would have tried to leave me if not for you. Her death is all your fault. You know what I'm after. Where is it? And where is my son?"

It was telling, in her mind, that he asked for his son second. This was a man who was incapable of love. If he wanted Mikey, it wasn't due to fatherly affection but for some twisted purpose of his own.

He yanked on her hair again. Even as spots danced

in front of her eyes, hope filled her heart. He had no idea where Mikey was. Which meant Leah had managed to hide him.

A meaty fist slammed into her jaw. Elise slumped to the floor as Hudson threw her back from him. He stepped toward her, rage written all over him. *I don't want to die yet.*

Hudson stopped suddenly as sirens filled the air. Blue-and-red strobe lights splashed across her eggshell-colored walls. The police had arrived. Fury flickered on his face. "I'll be back. I'll find it. And Michael. And then you're going to pay for what you've cost me."

Running, he headed for the back of the house. She heard the back door crash open.

She should move. Get up and tell the police…

Her thoughts were hazy, and she couldn't keep them together. She attempted to lift her head. It was too heavy. She lay there among the glass, knowing it was digging into her but unable to move.

Her eyes drifted shut.

A hand touched her neck.

Her pulse stuttered. Had he come back? She should fight. She forced her eyes open and met concerned eyes the color of melted chocolate. She blinked slowly. Short, medium brown hair. Strong jaw. And a dark blue LaMar Pond Police Department uniform came into view.

She was safe. For now. Her eyes drifted shut again.

Sergeant Ryan Parker stared down at the woman lying on the glass-covered area rug. It was hard to tell how badly she was wounded. Her jaw was bruised and starting to swell. She was bleeding from a half-dozen small cuts. He could clearly see shards of broken glass threaded in her golden-brown curls. He pressed two fingers to her pale throat again. Through his latex gloves, he could still feel a steady pulse.

"Hey, I know her. That's Elise St. Clair, the head dispatcher. Is she alive?"

Ryan looked up into the wide eyes and concerned face of his friend and colleague, Gavin Jackson. Ryan had recognized her, too, having seen her in town a few times. If she'd spoken, he knew her voice would have been instantly familiar since he'd spoken with her on the radio plenty of times. But she wasn't speaking now. Instead, she was lying frighteningly still.

He'd never actually been close enough to see the spatter of freckles on her nose before. She had never exactly encouraged personal interactions. She'd always been polite but somewhat detached, whether they spoke on the radio during work or in passing when they saw each other in town. In fact, he'd always gotten the distinct impression that she was somewhat antisocial. "Yeah, she's alive. Her pulse feels strong."

"That's good. The woman behind the table is dead." Jackson's voice was calm, but Ryan knew him well enough to see the rage brewing in his eyes. He hated when they arrived too late to protect someone in danger. They both did. "Looks like she was hit with the bat over against the wall. Are the paramedics here yet?"

As if summoned by his words, the paramedics walked through the door. Ryan and Jackson backed up, letting them do their job. The two officers started to leave the room, intending to search the rest of the house. Ryan let Jackson go ahead of him. He felt bad for his colleague, had seen the tight set of his eyes. He was taking this case personally.

Ryan wondered if Jackson had ever flirted with the young dispatcher. It wouldn't have surprised him to find out that he had. Oh, not that he suspected there was anything serious between them. There never was. For all his flirting and charm, Jackson didn't date. Ryan had a suspicion that he'd been burned badly before, but it wasn't his place to ask. If his friend wanted to talk about it, he would. When he was ready.

What was he doing, wasting time? He shook his head, dismayed at his lack of focus. He should be recording the scene. He had turned on his body camera before entering the house. The department had only received the cameras in the past month, so he was still getting used to using them. Finished in his current room, he carefully backed out of the scene. There were other rooms to check out, and he was only in the paramedics' way in here. He had started toward the stairs when a sudden thrashing made him halt. The woman cried out.

Ryan hurried back to where Elise was struggling against the paramedics.

"Ma'am, you need to calm down…"

She paid them no heed. In fact, her struggling increased. Ryan could see the wild panic in her smoky hazel eyes. He insinuated himself next to the first paramedic, Seth Travis. He had no plan, no idea of how he could help, but he had to try.

Those beautiful eyes fastened on him. She lurched forward slightly, grabbing his hand in both of hers and holding on to it tightly. Even injured, her grip was strong. Glancing down at their joined hands, he noted hers were scratched up, no doubt from the glass on the floor. Returning his gaze to Elise, he noted that some of the panic seemed to leach from her as she focused on him.

"Please." Her voice was husky, strained. "You need to find them. She has Mikey, but they're not safe. He won't stop looking for them. My nephew's missing. Babysitter's dead. You need to find my baby."

Them? Who else was missing? Her words weren't making sense. Farther into the room, he was aware of the coroner arriving. The crime scene was now officially a contaminated mess, but that couldn't be helped. Not when there was an injured woman on the premises and a child missing. And possibly some-one else.

Before he could ask her about it, her gaze flashed to the wall. He tracked it. "Oh, no!"

A dark wooden picture frame was placed centrally on the wall, clearly in a place of honor. Unlike all the other picture frames in the room, this one was undam-aged. It was also empty. Whatever picture had been inside it was gone.

"He's got Mikey's picture. He'll know what he looks like. She needs to hide," Elise murmured. Then her eyes rolled back in her head and she slumped, her hands relaxing and sliding off his. Just in time to miss the coroner and the paramedics hefting the covered stretcher and removing the other woman's body from the crime scene. As much as he hated having Elise fall unconscious, that was a sight he wouldn't want anyone to witness.

Within moments, the paramedics reentered the room and moved to his side to start loading Elise on a stretcher to transport her to the hospital. He saw both of them shooting him worried glances. He knew what they were thinking because his thoughts were there, too.

Oh, man. Did they have a kidnapping on their hands? Or was there an injured child on the premises? And what did her last statement mean?

"Jackson!" he shouted over his shoulder. Almost immediately, running footsteps answered him.

"Parker, got something?" Jackson halted in the doorway, his eyes sweeping around the room, looking for whatever had prompted the shout.

Ryan looked back at the woman on the stretcher. She was still out.

"She said something about needing to find her nephew. And maybe there was another person—female, I think—who needed to hide and who might have the child."

Jackson's eyes narrowed. "Sounds like she knew the person who attacked her."

"Yeah. That's my gut feeling, too. Whatever the case, we have at least one, maybe two, people at risk here, including a child."

Jackson was already turning. "On it."

"Seth," Ryan addressed the paramedic next to him. "I'm going to help search for the kid."

"Right." Seth kept his focus on the unconscious woman. "We're going to load her up in the ambulance. We'll hang out for a few minutes while you see if there's a child we need to transport."

Ryan acknowledged the comment with a wave, then he took off on his search of the house. He walked from room to room, keeping his service weapon out just in case he ran into their mysterious intruder. Jackson met him at the stairs.

"No baby up here, Parker. Toddler bed in the room at the end. Looks as if it's been searched, but nothing appears damaged. Toys and clothes suggest a child of about two or three. But there's no sign of him here."

Ryan frowned. "I don't know, Jackson. This whole scenario is just plain weird. It definitely wasn't a simple robbery. Plus, Elise seems to know something about the intruder. I won't know what until she regains consciousness and we can question her."

Jackson dipped his chin, acknowledging the truth of the statement. "Better let her get to the hospital first. Get checked out. I want to see if I can find a purse, something that can identity the dead woman. If that fails, I will check the scanner to see if we can find out who she is."

The marvels of technology. The LaMar Pond Police Department had also been equipped recently with automatic license plate–recognition scanners. The system alerted them if they passed a car with a flag on it. But they could also scan a car in emergency situations like this to get the information they needed on the registered owner. While it was handy, Ryan hated knowing he and Jackson would soon be notifying someone that their loved one had been murdered. That was one part of his job that he despised. His father would say it was one more reason to quit and do what he was meant to do. He and his dad didn't see eye to eye on many issues. His chosen career was one of them. But he had his reasons for why he had walked away from his family's ambitions for him. Reasons that would eat at him forever if betrayed his calling to make peace with his dad.

"Where's that breeze coming from?" Ryan pivoted on his heel and followed the cool draft that had teased the back of his neck. The room at the end of the hall was dim, but he could make out the sheer curtains blowing inward. Cautiously, weapon drawn, he edged the door open and turned on the light. The room was empty.

"Looks like someone climbed out the window."

Ryan nodded. "That's my take on it, too."

Stepping up to the window, he peered out. Someone had clearly jumped out the first-story window. He could see the boot prints in the mud along the side of the house. Small feet. Smaller than he'd expect from a man. Certainly not a man big enough to take Elise down so easily. She had to be five foot nine, if he had to guess, and while she was slender, she looked far from fragile. No, he was confident that those footprints had been made by someone other than their perp.

Jackson whistled.

Ryan jerked his head in his friend's direction. "What?"

He followed Jackson's finger as it pointed. A piece of gray cloth was hanging on a nail just outside the window. It was wet from the rain, but other than that it was clean and didn't look weathered, so it couldn't have been there long.

"Okay. Someone obviously went out this window." Urgency trickled through him. Decision time. "The kid's not here. Worst-case scenario, whoever attacked Elise and killed the other woman had an accomplice who got the child and fled out this window." He re-called Elise's words. "But Elise said *she* had Mikey and that *he* won't stop looking. That makes it sound like the woman and man weren't working together. So maybe it was someone else in the house who took the kid and ran with him? Let's give Seth the go-ahead to transfer Elise to the hospital. Then we'll finish here. We have to notify the chief, too. Let him know we have a possible abduction."

"Sounds like a plan. How about I continue here, and you go release the ambulance?"

Ryan gave him a thumbs-up, then strode out to where Seth and his partner were waiting. The rain had stopped while they were inside. As soon as he gave them the all clear, Seth swung up into the cab.

"I'll come to check up on her later," Ryan said. "Hopefully she'll be conscious and able to answer some questions for me."

The ambulance started back down the long drive-way, swaying as it moved along the uneven surface. Ryan watched it turn onto the road and disappear, then he went out to the cruiser and pulled up the in-formation on the car sitting next to the garage. When the driver's license of Diana Mosher, age forty-two, popped up, he knew he'd found the identity of the babysitter. With a sigh, he snatched up his cell phone and put a call into Chief Kennedy. It was picked up on the second ring.

"Chief Kennedy here," said the voice on the other end, a hint of a drawl present.

"Parker, sir." Ryan watched as Jackson moved out-side to check the perimeter. "Jackson and I are at the house of Elise St. Clair, the dispatcher. We got a call a little before four this afternoon that there had been a possible break-in here. A Ms. Diana Mosher, her babysitter, was found dead at the scene. Elise herself was unconscious. She's been roughed up and just left in the ambulance. She has a child, age approximately two or three—we still don't have specifics. He's missing, and there's evidence that someone escaped out a first-floor window. Possibly an accomplice, although I suspect from Elise's remarks before she passed out that there might have been someone here when the house was broken into who ran with the child to hide him. If that's the case, then that woman would be in danger, as well."

A soft sigh of regret came through the phone. "A shame about Diana. She was an art teacher at the elementary school last year. I'll go talk to the medical examiner and notify her next of kin. What's Elise St. Clair's condition?"

"Unsure, sir. She was out when the ambulance left. Jackson and I are finishing here at the scene. We have to finish checking the rest of the house and the garage. Then we'll proceed to the hospital. We need to talk to her as soon as she wakes up."

"Understood."

Ryan hung up the phone and replaced it in his pocket. He couldn't quite stem the feeling that Elise was not out of danger. He let his eyes follow the trail of destruction in the room where they'd found her. Not a thing had been touched except for the dozens of pictures that had lined the mantel and hung on the walls. Even the couple of pictures sitting on top of the bookcase in the corner had been shattered. No, this was not some random attack by a stranger. This was personal. A deliberate attack against the pretty young woman that no one seemed to know much about.

That needed to change. He needed to get to her and find out everything he could about the elusive dispatcher. Her life—and possibly the lives of two others, including a small child—depended on it.

TWO

Twenty minutes later, a second cruiser arrived. Two officers emerged from it.

"Hey, Parker," the young officer said, toting a large camera. "We're here to assist."

When the officers had everything under control, he grabbed Jackson. He needed to talk with Elise and get whatever information she could provide.

Ryan dropped Jackson off at the police station to get a head start on the paperwork before continuing to the hospital. He parked his cruiser in the visitor lot, leaving the spaces nearest the building free for those who were patients or family members. It was still light out, but just barely. A few fat droplets hit his windshield, signaling the start of a new rain shower. Light and wet. He grimaced. He left his vehicle and ducked his head to keep the water out of his face as he strode to the awning-covered entrance. The sliding-glass doors hissed as they opened.

The nurse at the ER desk directed him to the room where Elise had been moved to for observation. Relief flooded him. Her injuries had not been severe enough to require surgery. After thanking the woman politely, he headed down the hall to the room she'd indicated.

The door opened as he approached. A nurse walked out. He flashed his badge, even though his uniform clearly identified him as a police officer. She pursed her lips.

"I know you have to question her, but please remember she's been injured and traumatized. She needs rest."

"Yes, ma'am."

He stood in the doorway for a moment, watching Elise as she lay there, her eyes closed. He was reluctant to disturb her even while knowing that he would. Her golden-brown hair flowed back from a small widow's peak, moving into a rambling mass of corkscrew curls. Hair that would have been the envy of his sisters, who had used any number of curlers and curling irons through the years to style their naturally stick-straight hair. Her skin was bruised and cut in various places. The rest of her skin had a faint golden tan. The freckles he'd noticed earlier stood out against the bridge of her nose.

She stirred.

Ryan stepped fully into the room, clearing his throat gently.

Her eyes flared open, alarm flashing in their dusky hazel depths.

"Hey, hey! It's okay." He laid a calming hand on her shoulder, praying she wouldn't tear out the IV in her panic. When she calmed, he removed his hand. "I'm Sergeant Ryan Parker. Remember me? I found you at your house today."

"Parker..." she breathed. Her voice had a gentle rasp

to it. She stopped struggling but didn't relax. He could see her trying to put the pieces together in her mind. "Yes, I remember you. We've met a few times." Her eyes closed briefly. A tear slipped out from beneath her lashes. "I came home. He was there. Mikey—"

Her breathing hitched. He touched her shoulder again.

"Easy, Elise. I need to know what happened, but I want you to stay as calm as possible while you tell me. Start at the beginning. I know it's hard, but you have to give me everything you can." He kept his voice soft, using what his youngest sister always called his "comfort voice."

"I know. I know. I'm just so scared." Elise's voice cracked. Another tear slipped out the corner of her eye and slid into her hair. She drew in a deep breath and let it out slowly, shuddering. "I can do this."

Ryan stepped back from the bed and lowered himself into the chair at her side. Before he could start his questions, the door opened and a nurse entered. The woman frowned slightly when she saw Ryan, but she didn't make a fuss as she checked Elise's readings. He waited, beginning only after she had left.

"Who's Mikey?"

"Mikey is my nephew. I have raised him since my sister was murdered. He's three."

He could see her emotions were rising to the surface again. And no wonder. A sister murdered and now her nephew missing. Sympathy filled him. He couldn't imagine what she was going through, but right now he needed to know what had transpired.

"Tell me what happened this afternoon. Dispatch said there was a break-in."

She was silent a moment. Her eyes were closed as she pulled herself together, but he knew she wasn't sleeping. Her breath hitched as she struggled to control her emotions. "I was at work when I got a call at the 911 center. It was from my babysitter's phone, but it wasn't Diana. It was the girl who cleans my house. She was screaming. I couldn't understand everything she said. She's Amish and was talking in Pennsylvania Dutch at the beginning. Then she switched to English and said she thought that my babysitter was dead. Then she got quiet and said she thought she heard someone still in the house. I rushed out, told my coworker to notify the police and send an ambulance and then I headed home. When I got there, she was gone and so was my nephew."

"Your cleaning girl?" He sat up. The image of the small footsteps flashed through his brain. It would make sense.

She nodded, her brow wrinkling as if she were in pain. "Leah Byler. She comes every week. I think she has Mikey. Please. We have to find them."

Byler. Amish. He remembered the gray material stuck on the nail. Things were beginning to make sense. "I will make finding her and your nephew top priority, I promise. Right now, though, I need you to finish walking me through the events, okay?"

The sigh she released was impatient, but she nodded.

"So someone broke into your house—"

"No. Not someone. *Him.* My murdering brother-in-law."

He blinked. That was some pretty unequivocal language. "When you say 'murdering,' are you saying that literally?"

Elise tried to sit up, grimaced, then managed to pull herself higher up on her pillows. "Yes, literally. Two and a half years ago, I was staying with my sister. She'd recently kicked her husband out after a fight between them." She sighed. "Things had been bad between them for a while. He was controlling, aggressive. He yelled at her all the time. She said he didn't hit her…but I didn't believe her. My sister wasn't clumsy, and yet she always seemed to have bruises. Especially on her neck. He always went for the neck." Elise's eyes filled with tears again, and she angrily brushed them away.

"I tried to get her to leave so many times, but she seemed more scared of leaving than of staying. Then Mikey was born—that was when things finally changed. She had put up with the abuse when it was just aimed at her. When he started turning that anger toward their baby, she decided she'd had enough and kicked him out."

Ryan grimaced. He'd seen this far too often in his work—women who put up with habitual abuse. He was glad that Elise's sister had been strong enough to put a stop to things to protect her child.

"I think we both expected him to come back in a day or two, drunk and belligerent, so I went to stay with her for a while," Elise continued. "She was scared to be at the house by herself. But he never came. After a few days, she tried tracking him down, but it was like he'd disappeared. She couldn't find him…"

"I thought you said your brother-in-law was after you?"

Boy, did he get the stink eye for that one.

"If you're through interrupting…" Her voice could

freeze the air between them. Despite the seriousness of the situation, he was amused. This woman was not easily intimidated, that was sure.

"Yeah. Sorry. Go on."

A regal nod, and she continued. "As I was saying, he was missing for a while. Then the police came and said that he had apparently been killed. His car caught on fire after some kind of explosion and was totally destroyed. His body was never found. I was relieved for my sister that he was truly gone, but it bothered me that they didn't find a corpse."

"It's not that unusual," Ryan told her. "Especially if the fire was as bad as you said."

"Yes, I know that—but even then, I wondered if there was more to it. After he'd left, Karalynne had found evidence that her husband was into something bad, like in a mob or something. I got worried because it seemed like something he would do—fake his death so that he could get away from the trouble he'd created for himself, not caring about the consequences to anyone else. My sister was terrified. She didn't know what he was involved in, but if it was bad enough to get him killed then she worried that she might not be safe. She was waiting for whoever might have killed him to come after her next."

Ryan scooted to the front of his seat. There was more to this tale, he could feel it coming. Elise had gone pale again, and her breathing was quicker. Her eyes skittered to the closed door. The woman was practically jumping out of her skin from nerves. Why?

"Elise." He brought her eyes back to his. "You're safe here."

"I know. I know. I'm sorry." She brushed her short

wispy bangs back with her left hand. The sight of her bruised cheek infuriated him. "Karalynne had found some evidence, like I said."

"What did she find?"

"A box hidden in their crawl space with cash…a lot of it. The box also had a couple of phones—the cheap, pay-as-you-go kind. And a gun."

Her next words were almost a whisper. He had to strain to hear them.

"A few days later, I came home, and she was all agitated. She had gotten up her nerve and searched through his things more carefully. This time, she found something that terrified her. Hard evidence on an SD card. She wouldn't tell me what was on it, said I was safer not knowing. I told her she had to go to the police. Because even if Hudson was dead, he'd probably been working with others and this evidence could help the authorities make a case, stop these people from being a threat to her and Mikey and anyone else."

"Did she?"

Elise shrugged. "I never knew. I stayed with her for another week. When nothing happened, she settled down and told me to go home. I did, even though I was worried for her. Two weeks later, I got a call from the neighbor across the hall. Karalynne been mugged, the neighbor said, and was dead. If she'd been shot or stabbed, or even had fallen and hit her head or something, I might have believed it really was just a random mugging. Or maybe even Hudson's associates coming after her, as she'd feared. But that wasn't how she died."

"How did she die?"

Elise's hazel eyes stared straight into his as she answered. "Strangled. Hudson always did go for the neck."

Ryan reared back. "You think he killed her?"

She slumped back against the pillows. "I know it seems crazy. I just couldn't get the idea out of my head. I shared my suspicions with the police, but it was obvious they didn't believe me. I told them about the box Elise had found, and the SD card, too, but they couldn't find any of it in the house. Which meant they couldn't do anything about Hudson or his associates. I got custody of Mikey and moved here."

Oh, man. What a heartbreaking story. He frowned. "I get that the coincidence is weird. Your sister being attacked after finding evidence against her husband, and especially her being strangled. But it really could be a coincidence. Why are you so convinced he's alive?"

Elise reached out and grabbed his hand. He winced. Although he doubted she was aware of it, her nails were digging into his skin. Ignoring the sensation, he kept his eyes trained on the lovely woman lying on the hospital bed.

"I saw him."

"Who?"

Elise tightened her grip. "Today, when I went home. I saw him. Hudson. He was there in my house. I think he really was in the car accident—it wasn't faked. But he survived. And now he's after he. He hit me. And said he'd come for his son. He blamed me for Karalynne kicking him out. Promised to kill me. And he demanded that I tell him where to find Mikey and where *it* was."

A punch in the gut would have been more pleasant than hearing about some monster gunning for this woman and a poor child.

"What does he think you have?"

He had a hunch, but didn't want to put ideas into her head.

"Isn't it obvious? He thinks I have the SD card. I don't—she never gave it to me. She must have hidden it. If he can get rid of the evidence that links him to any crime, and of me, then what would stop him from coming back and starting over somewhere else?"

He tapped his chin. "He obviously wanted his son back, also, enough to risk coming back from the dead. Why take the chance to confront you?"

Anxiety washed over her face. "And every moment I'm in here, he could be getting closer to Mikey."

Ryan leaned forward, letting her see his eyes, hoping to convince her of his sincerity. "Elise, we'll do everything we can to find Mikey. I need to know about Leah. Does she have family nearby?"

Her brow furrowed in thought. "I think she lives with her cousin. Pretty sure her parents passed away. She's sixteen."

Sixteen and possibly being hunted by a killer. Oh, man. The department would have to work fast on this one. And she was Amish, so there would be no pictures of her.

"Can you give me a description of her?"

Elise squeezed her eyes shut. "She's probably around five-two or -three. Her hair is light brown. It looks straight, but I can't say for sure. Brown eyes. Slender, but not skinny. Sharp chin."

He questioned her for another minute or so, trying to get any detail that he could share.

A few minutes later, he left Elise's room, feeling the burden of holding so many lives in his hands.

She couldn't remember the last time she'd felt so cold. Like she'd never be warm again. And it wasn't just temperature cold, either. Sitting in a sterile hospital room, with an IV hooked into her arm and monitors surrounding her, she felt she'd woken up in someone else's nightmare. But it was all hers.

Did Sergeant Ryan Parker believe her? It was so hard to tell. He had finished questioning her and then left the room, supposedly to give a better description of Leah and Mikey to those searching. Fortunately, he'd been thoughtful enough to retrieve her purse from her car, and she had pictures of her adorable nephew on her phone. He had promised to return as soon as things were settled.

She wasn't sure if he bought the story about Hudson. It was all the truth, but how was he to know it? She'd been attacked, and he might conclude that the terror of it had her mind playing tricks on her, making her believe her attacker was her brother-in-law simply because he was the man in her past she feared the most. And as for the reasons she'd had to fear Hudson in the past, she hadn't told anyone about her brother-in-law...not about his brutal temper, or his charismatic personality. Nothing. And now Diana was dead. In retrospect, she had been trying to wipe him from their lives.

Seeing him today had been a shock. Even knowing in her soul that he'd survived the car crash and that he was responsible for Karalynne's death, still she hadn't been prepared. How had such a cruel, malicious man tricked her sweet sister into falling in love with him? And then to father such a beautiful little boy like Mikey...

Where had Leah taken Mikey? Was he cold, too? Hungry?

Leah hadn't known anything about the monster searching for her, but the girl had known the danger was real. The fear in her voice during that phone call had proved that much. Elise had to hold on to the belief that the Amish girl had taken her nephew somewhere safe. Worry rattled in her heart for Leah's family. Ryan would protect them, wouldn't he? But how much could he do?

What if Hudson had found them already? Leah couldn't have gotten too far on foot, and Hudson was a very large man. It would have taken so little for him to overpower her and...

No, no, no! She was not going to give in to her fear and despair. She'd talked to the Amish girl enough times to take her measure. Leah was a hard worker and she was clever, and she knew the woods and roads around this town much better than Hudson ever would.

The door creaked open, Elise tensed. For a moment, all she could think was that he had found her again. She slumped back against the stiff pillow when Ryan's headed popped around the door. After he observed that she was awake, he opened the door and let himself fully into the room. She allowed her eyes to skim his face, his posture, searching for any clue of doubt or skepticism. The masculine face above her gave nothing away. The bland expression could have meant anything. All too well she remembered the pitying looks she'd received from the Chicago police when she'd insisted that Karalynne had been murdered by her husband.

She remembered one officer saying, "No matter how much you didn't like the man, miss, he's dead. You need to accept that."

Oh, how she had wanted to scream! They had no idea what that man was capable of, the lengths he would go to in order to deceive and get his way.

Not like the officer standing in front of her. Ryan was the antithesis of Hudson. Strong. Honest. And way too handsome for his own good. She shook her head. She didn't have time for those thoughts. Plus, her experience with Brady had taught her caution. Even thinking of her ex-fiancé was painful, so she shoved those memories away.

Peeking under the fringe of her bangs, she watched the handsome sergeant. Well, he wasn't giving off any condescending vibes, as if he thought she was too irrational to give an accurate report of what had happened.

None of this was important. Whether or not he believed her didn't matter. The only thing that mattered was the safety of Mikey and Leah. Once again, she sent a prayer up for their safety. Part of her wondered if it did any good.

Sorry, God. After all He'd pulled her through, she wouldn't allow herself to doubt Him now.

Ryan grabbed the chair closest to the bed and dragged it six inches closer before seating himself next to her. A flush rose in her cheeks at his intense scrutiny. She squirmed, uncomfortable. A snarky comment rose to her lips. She bit them to hold it in. Sarcasm was a natural defense for her, but it probably wouldn't be wise to use it in the current situation.

Instead, she waited him out. Surely, he'd say something eventually. The wait just about gave her hives, but she forced herself to be patient.

"Okay," he finally said. His voice was soft, with a firm edge to it. The kind of voice people instinctively quieted down to listen to. She realized she had leaned in his direction to catch his voice. Embarrassed, she made herself sit back. "I have an Amber Alert out for your nephew," he said. "As Leah is Amish, I have no pictures to send out, but that can't be helped. At least we have your description."

Elise felt a frown work its way across her face.

"I wish we could get a picture out. I'm sure that Leah will protect Mikey, but I would feel a whole lot better if the police were able to find them before—" she stopped herself from mentioning Hudson's name "—before my attacker does."

A flicker of doubt crossed his lean face. Was he doubting her story? She braced herself to be shut down again.

"Elise, I talked with the police who dealt with your sister's death. Are you positive your attacker today was Hudson Langor?"

Hot waves of anger started to swirl in her gut. She opened her mouth, then shut it. Ryan's expression wasn't one of disbelief. Would he give her a chance?

"Yes, it was Hudson. I'd recognize his voice anywhere. Even though he doesn't look anything like the man I knew, his voice is the same. It's a very distinctive voice. And the things he said… He blamed me for his problems with his wife, demanded that I turn over his son. Why would anyone other than Hudson say those things? He wants me dead. And the evidence he thinks I have against him. And his son. In that order."

He placed his hands on his thighs and pushed to his feet. "If you're sure, that's good enough for me. I guess you'd know the man if you came face-to-face with him."

"I would. You might not, though."

"Huh?" His brow wrinkled quizzically.

"He's changed. The face I saw earlier today was not the same as the one I had known. He's been through a fire. I'm guessing it's from the car accident that supposedly killed him. Or something worse. But his eyes and his voice, they were the same."

"So you're saying…?"

"I'm saying that you could have his picture right in front of you and still not recognize him."

He rubbed his hand down his face. "Well, that adds a new level of complicated to this case. Hold on. I have an idea."

Turning on his heel, Ryan went to the door and opened it, yanking his phone out of his pocket as he walked. She didn't know whether to be amused or dismayed at his abrupt exit. The moment she heard the door click shut behind him, though, fear for her nephew swamped her again.

In a short time, it would be dark. Mikey was terrified of the dark. He had a special night-light and a specific stuffed animal at home to help him sleep. Now he had neither.

She couldn't stay here! She had to go out and find

him! The police had a vague idea what Leah looked like, but not a definitive image. And who knew how close Hudson was? That thought drove her on.

Sucking in her breath against the pain that flared with every movement, Elise pushed back the covers and twisted to move her legs over the edge of the bed, intent on escaping.

THREE

"Hey, what do you think you're doing?"

Ryan dashed back into the room, appalled to find Elise swaying beside her bed. He hadn't meant to shout, but seeing her bloodless face and huge eyes starting to roll backward had shaken him to the core. He was amazed she wasn't flat on her face.

The nurse rushed in after him, no doubt alerted by his shout. Her face puckered in disapproval. She made tsking sounds with her tongue, urgently moving to settle her patient back in bed. "Miss St. Clair! You are in no condition to be moving about! The doctor gave you some medication that will make you drowsy. You have to let it wear off."

Elise did not return to bed quietly.

"I have to leave! My nephew is in trouble. He needs me." Her voice was hoarse. Ryan could see that the effort of getting to her feet was already draining her energy. She sagged against the edge of the bed and finally allowed the nurse to tuck her back under the covers. Just what he needed. Not only did he have a child and an Amish teenager to find, he had an over-zealous aunt determined to risk her own health and safety. Even though she could barely walk. He had to admire her grit, though. Judging by the pallor of her skin, she was in considerable pain. If he'd been the doctor his father wanted him to be, maybe he could have helped her deal with that.

But God had wanted him to be a police officer. There was no going back on that decision.

"Elise, enough." He strode closer until he was directly in front of her. "You need to let me do my job. I will find Mikey. But you need to remain in the hospital until the doctor releases you."

"Which is not going to be tonight," the nurse interjected.

Elise huffed out an annoyed breath. There was a storm brewing inside her, that was for certain. Hopefully, he could persuade her to accept his plan.

"Ryan, I'm the only one here who knows what Leah looks like. It makes sense for me to help."

He couldn't help it. The sarcastic snort left his mouth before he could stop it.

She opened her mouth, no doubt to argue. He didn't know her that well, but he had already learned that she was bone stubborn. And since he was the one who was literally standing between her and what she wanted at the moment, that meant he was going to get the brunt of it. Shoving his hands into his pockets, he waited for her argument. None came. Instead, her eyes widened as she caught sight of something over his shoulder.

Reflexes had him spinning to face whatever she had seen. He came face-to-face with the grinning countenance of his friend, Sergeant Miles Olsen. Miles was holding the hand of his pretty wife, Rebecca. Rebecca had grown up in an Amish family.

She'd chosen to leave before being baptized, which meant that even though she didn't live in the Amish community, she still had a relationship with her family. When Ryan had asked Miles about Leah Byler, he had responded that Rebecca had known her, although not well. Leah's family wasn't originally from the community where Rebecca's family lived.

"Good, you're here." It was about time. He could use some reinforcements.

"Hey, Parker. No problem. Always glad to help." Miles nodded, and his floppy blond bangs bounced on his forehead. Miles always looked like an overgrown Boy Scout. Until he got into serious police mode. Then his demeanor could be as fierce as any other officer's.

"What's going on?" Elise's soft, husky voice was rife with suspicion.

"Nothing to get worked up about." He walked back to her side so he could look down at her. Man, she was pretty. Wait, where had that come from? That thought did not belong in his head right now. "This is Sergeant Miles Olsen, and his wife, Rebecca."

Her eyes focused in on the couple. He was surprised to note that she didn't gawk when Miles started signing to his wife. Rebecca was deaf, and Miles often served as her interpreter with the hearing community. Some people had a problem with it and found it embarrassing to be around her. Others reacted like it was the most fascinating sight they'd ever encountered. Elise didn't seem to be bothered at all. Good for her.

"Okay. It's nice to meet you both. So why are you here?"

Miles smiled at her. He signed while he spoke.

"Ryan said that your nephew was probably with Leah Byler. We know her. Or at least Rebecca does."

Rebecca nodded and started signing, her slim hands flashing too fast for Ryan to catch every movement. Fortunately, Miles was far more experienced at this, and interpreted. "Yes, I know Leah. She moved here recently from New Wilmington and is staying with her cousin. I talked with the bishop of the community. Normally, no pictures are allowed—either photographs or drawings. However, since a child is at risk, he made an exception this once and gave me permission to do this."

Rebecca reached deep inside the bag she had slung over her shoulder. Elise gasped when the blonde woman pulled out a hand-drawn image of an Amish teenager with brown hair. It was a profile picture, not a full image. But Elise recognized the subject instantly, which gave her hope that maybe it would be good enough for a stranger to recognize her. And if she had a toddler with her, it would make her all the more memorable.

"That's Leah! Did you just draw that, from memory?" Elise leaned forward, squinting as she took in the image on the paper.

"Yes. I am not sure if I got the eyes right."

Elise beckoned with her left hand, the one not hampered by the IV. Rebecca moved in closer to the bed. Ryan edged away to let them have room.

"I think the eyes are pretty close. At least it will give the police a good idea of who they are looking for."

Ryan peered at Elise. There was a faint flush in her cheeks, dispelling the sickly appearance she'd had at first. Her voice was livelier, too. He knew what he was seeing. Hope. A sudden dread clenched his heart. He did not want to fail this woman, to watch the hope fade into anguish. He'd disappointed far too many people in his life.

Stop it! He mentally shook himself out of his morose thoughts, like a dog shaking off the water after a swim, sending his doubts flying. He had no room for them. Those insecurities—that was his father speaking. The father who never talked with him without expressing his disappointment that Ryan hadn't followed both his parents and his older brother into the field of medicine.

You could have made something of yourself, Ryan. That was his father's favorite refrain.

It didn't matter, though. Medicine was not his calling. He had known since high school what he was meant to do with his life. And if God approved, well, his family was just going to have to learn to accept it.

Which didn't make his father's disappointment any easier to bear. He shrugged his shoulders, mentally pulling himself back to the crisis at hand. Now wasn't the time for nostalgia.

Now was the time for action.

"If the picture is accurate, then I will send it out. It will be easier to search if we know who we are searching for. I will also use the pictures you've given me of Mikey and circulate them. We have already put out an Amber Alert on him." After pulling his phone from his pocket, he scanned the drawing with an app, then forwarded it. He thought of something. "I will also pull up your brother-in-law's photo from the DMV and send that out."

She raised her eyebrows. "Okay. But I already told you, it won't do you any good. He doesn't look the same now. I wouldn't have recognized him if I hadn't heard him speak."

"So noted."

Ryan thought for a moment. She needed to speak with a photographic artist. Unfortunately, the woman the department normally hired was out of town for a few days. They didn't have the time to wait. He excused himself from the room and went to call his chief.

"Chief Kennedy here." His deep drawl might have sounded casual, but that was deceptive. Ryan knew that the chief was solid and would give his all to see justice done.

"It's Parker, sir. I am at the hospital with Miss St. Clair. She says the man who attacked her is her brother-in-law. He was reported to have died in an accident a few years back, but no body was ever found. Apparently, he was changed by the accident, but his voice is the same—and he spoke about things only her brother-in-law would know. So if it's not him, someone has worked very hard to put on a convincing act."

There was a pause. "Well, most people know their own relatives. Therefore, I will assume for the moment that the man in question is not dead, but is in fact here in LaMar Pond. What do you need, Sergeant?"

"Sir, she says that his appearance has been altered drastically. I have Olsen and his wife here with me—"

"And you'd like Rebecca to draw a current image since our sketch artist is unavailable, am I correct?"

Ryan let out a breath. "Yes, sir."

"I don't have a problem with that, Parker. If anyone says anything about it not being official, I'll accept the blame."

"Thanks."

Ryan popped back into the room. Elise was exhausted, he could tell. This couldn't wait, however. Besides, even if he left her alone to rest, he very much doubted that she'd be able to sleep. Not with her nephew and Leah missing.

The moment he entered the room, the quiet conversation the others had been having ceased. Elise speared him with her hazel eyes so full of hope it caught him off guard. The weight of the trust she had in him pressed down on him. What if he failed her? *Lord, let me be Your instrument. Help me to bring the child back to her and keep all of them safe.*

In a few quick words, he explained his plan. They all agreed. Ryan pulled up Langor's image from the DMV database and sent it to Rebecca's phone. Using that as a starting point, Rebecca began to gather the information about what changes needed to be made for an accurate sketch while Miles acted as her interpreter. Half an hour later, Rebecca handed him the updated image of Hudson Langor. Glancing between the two, he whistled. Elise was right. He would have walked right past him and not even known.

A few minutes later, Miles and Rebecca left. Ryan took a few minutes to get the sketches sent out. Better get the search started now. Who knew how far away the girl was with the child. Or if the pyscho brother-in-law had made any progress in his quest. He hoped not. There wasn't much more he could do tonight.

His other concern was that the man seemed to feel Elise was a loose end that needed to be eradicated.

Ah, well. At least she was in the hospital for the
night. There were nurses and doctors coming to check
on her throughout the night. He'd have a chat with security, before he left, to put them on alert. She should
be safe. Maybe she'd be able to get enough rest so that
she could remember something more, anything more,
that might help them figure out where her nephew and
the Amish girl had headed.

It had long since gone dark outside. The faint glow
of the moon splashed over the floor now. Even though
she knew it wasn't, it looked warm, as if touching it
would chase away some of the chill she was feeling
in her heart. It was a comforting glow, reminding her
that the Creator of everything was near. A twinge of
guilt pricked her conscience. She hadn't given God
much attention lately.

Elise sighed. She was stuck here, in this narrow,
uncomfortable hospital bed with a needle in her arm.
The doctor who'd checked her out had declared she
was dehydrated from her illness earlier that week. Sergeant Parker had left. Was he coming back? He hadn't
really said. It surprised her to realize that she was kind
of hoping the handsome officer would return.

She needed something to distract her thoughts.
Thinking about what could be happening out there
with Mikey was driving her crazy. Even though she
wasn't his mother, he was her baby. Her whole world
had revolved around the adorable boy with the dark
brown eyes and curly brown hair for over two years.
The ache inside her intensified as her imagination
pictured him cold or sick or scared. Phantom whim-
pers filled her ears.

Squeezing her eyes closed, she forced her thoughts to focus on something else.

Sergeant Parker's face flashed through her mind. The warmth in his chocolate-brown eyes. She especially liked his smile. It was unusual. Quirky. Kind of lopsided. He had a nice square jaw, too. When he had left, he had been sporting a slight five-o'clock shadow. She wondered what that roughness would feel like if she lifted her hand to his face. Her eyes popped open. That wasn't helping. Frankly, she was surprised her mind had even gone there. After everything that had happened with Brady, she'd been against even the idea of entering a relationship. Besides, taking care of Mikey had been her priority—he was the only male she had time for her in her life.

The door opened and the man himself entered the room. She flushed, embarrassed to have been thinking of him in such a way. She didn't even really know the man! True, she'd met him a time or two, and had been talking to him for two years on the radio, but that wasn't the same as actually spending time with a person.

"Hey, Elise. How ya doing?" He smiled slightly. Wow. He really did have a great smile, with the slightest hint of dimples appearing in his cheeks. She hadn't noticed that before.

Oh, wait. She needed to answer him.

"Been better. But I'm okay. Sergeant Parker—"

He cut her off. "Ryan. Please. What's on your mind?"

"I want to know what's happening. While you search, I mean. I don't want to be kept out of the loop." She held her breath. Would he brush her off? Tell her that police business was just that?

"I understand," he responded in his velvet voice. Her breath left her in a whoosh, she was so relieved. "I will give you all the details I can. In the meantime, I am going to leave for the night. First thing tomorrow morning, as soon as you are released, we have some planning to do."

"So no one will be looking for Mikey tonight?" She didn't like the sound of that.

"That's not what I said. The Amber Alert has gone out, along with the sketch of your brother-in-law, and back at the station several people are still looking into it. Checking on leads. But I need to get some sleep if I want to be able to function, and so do you." He turned to the door. "Good night. I will see you in the morning."

And he was gone.

She couldn't believe it. She was so worried she was ready to tear out her hair. And he'd just left! In all fairness, she didn't know what else he could do. The man wasn't a machine. He did say people were still searching. There really wasn't anything more that she could ask him to do.

Sighing, she lay against the pillows, trying to shift this way and that to find a comfortable position. She'd shut her eyes, then open them five minutes later. Her nerves started to get to her.

Her door was shut, but every once in a while she thought she heard footsteps stop at her door.

Was Hudson in the hall?

She strained to listen, trying to separate the different sounds outside the door. Her doorknob seemed to rattle slightly. Then it stopped. Goose bumps formed on her arms. A scream crawled up and lodged in her throat.

The footsteps moved away from the door.

Her night nurse entered to check her vitals. The woman was coolly professional, her voice soothing as she checked the IV and the monitors and made notes on the chart attached to the clipboard.

Feeling ridiculous for her fears, Elise forced herself to ask the woman the question that was screaming inside her mind. "Was there someone hanging around outside my door?"

The pitying glance the nurse gave her made her want to shrink down inside the blankets and hide.

"Honey, no one has been outside your door. You're completely safe here."

Elise grimaced. Well, at least she knew.

She thanked the woman and watched her leave.

At some point, she drifted off into an uneasy sleep. She woke up at one point when she dreamed that she heard Mikey crying out for her. There were tears on her lashes when she lifted them. Her head jerked around when her door opened. A male nurse entered wheeling a medicine cart in front of him. She glanced at the clock. Two thirty in the morning. Sighing, she gave the man a tired smile.

He didn't smile back.

Actually, he didn't even make eye contact. Feeling uneasy, she watched him look at her chart. Maybe he was just shy. Or not a social person. Whatever. She was not impressed with the bedside manners of the staff in this hospital. Owning to herself that she was being ridiculous, she shut her eyes again, listening to the sound of him moving around her room.

She opened one eye. He was watching her. The moment he caught her glance, he looked away and continued with his work.

Now she was frustrated—and annoyed with herself for her own frustration. The man was just here to do a job. He wasn't Hudson. Even with his changed appearance there was no way Hudson had shrunk five inches. She was starting to get paranoid.

Pressing her lips together, she closed her eyes again, determined to sleep. She could hear nurses talking right outside her door and did her best to block them. Finally, the voices drifted away.

A minute later, she felt the hairs on her arms stand on end. Her lids flew open.

The nurse was standing directly in front of her, a pillow held in both hands. He smiled. A grim, ugly little smile that made her blood curdle.

"Good night, lady. Nothing personal, you understand, but it appears someone doesn't like you."

The last thing she saw before he pushed the pillow down over her face was his horrific smirk. Then she gasped as the white linen pillowcase pressed against her nose. Her gasp was cut off as the ability to suck in air left her. Thrusting her arms upward, she pushed and shoved at the man smothering her. A twinge in her arm…her IV had pulled free.

She barely noticed the pain, instead focused on the screaming in her lungs as her last bit of air vanished in a silent scream. She was going to die.

FOUR

She could feel herself fading. Her burning lungs strained to grasp at air. Air that was barricaded by the hospital pillow held in place with grim, brutal strength. Desperate, she flailed her arms and twisted on the bed. He was so much stronger than she was. Her left hand banged against the bedside table. Her fingers brushed over something long and smooth.

And pointed at one end.

Grabbing on to it, she thrust it upward with all her remaining strength. Her wrist and forearm were jarred by the impact. That didn't matter. What was important was that her attacker yelled and the tension against her face eased. Pushing away the pillow, she scrambled over the opposite edge of the bed and stood on shaking legs that threatened not to hold her up. She sucked huge gulps of air into her aching lungs while keeping an eye on the man glaring at her. Small dark splotches dotted the side of his scrubs. Blood. The fork she'd plunged into his side was still hanging by one tine off the shirt. It looked bent.

His eyes, though, were what held her attention. They were full of murderous rage.

She backed away from the bed. There was nowhere to go. She was blocked in by the wall and machinery on her left. And on her right... He was between her and the door.

And he was coming to finish the job. As he rounded the bed, he pulled the mangled fork off his clothes and tossed it away from him. It clattered against the wall and fell to the floor. He came at her, hands raised and curved to grab her by the throat.

That was how her sister had died. She would *not* let it happen to her.

Elise leaped on top of the bed she'd just vacated and scooted across it. If she could get to the door...

Before she could move, he was around the bed again and coming at her.

Elise screamed as loud as she could.

It was choked off when two large hands circled her throat.

The door crashed open. Two nurses stood there. For a second, they gaped at the man with the bloody stains on his shirt before one of them yelled and they charged into the room. Elise couldn't keep track of who was yelling what while they attempted to subdue him. He shoved them aside and dashed out the open door, tripping over his own feet as he darted into the hallway. Elise heard more yelling and crashing, but couldn't tell what was happening from where she was. The nurses were bearing down on her, trying to coax her back to bed and to check on her condition. A young doctor scurried in, gave her a cursory exam, pronounced she was fine and instructed her to try to sleep and not to worry.

"Just try to relax," he said over his shoulder as he hurried out of the room.

Was he trying to be funny? Like that was even a possibility.

The two nurses beckoned her to lie down. She didn't want to, but complied, mostly because she felt bad that they looked so rattled. Like she wasn't? Still, she slipped under the thin blanket. But she drew the line at the IV.

"Absolutely not," she stated firmly. "Nor do I want any more pain meds messing with my mind, making me feel all fuzzy and confused."

No matter how the nurses coaxed, she wouldn't give in. Finally, they let her have her way. A new commotion outside the door had her sitting up. She sighed, relieved, when she noted that the police had arrived. It was about time. An unfamiliar police officer breezed in to question her. Where was Ryan?

Don't be ridiculous, Elise. The man has to sleep sometime, she reminded herself. He was a sergeant with the police department. He had an important job and responsibilities. He was not her personal bodyguard.

Still, she felt a bit bereft that he wasn't the one interviewing her. After a few questions, her chest grew tight and her belly quivered. What if this was a trick? That nurse had been a fraud. What if this officer was just another person sent to get her out of the way?

Elise shifted to the side on her bed, as far to the opposite edge as she dared without falling off the mattress. The officer gave her a quizzical glance. She froze. If he was legitimate, he was probably thinking that she was a little nuts. If he wasn't...

If he wasn't really a cop, she might have just tipped her hand and let him know she was onto him. Her muscles tightened. She needed to be ready to escape if he made a move toward her. Inching her hand closer to the edge of the blanket, she curled her fingers around it, ready to whip it away if necessary.

After the longest fifteen minutes of her life, he departed, saying he had all the information he needed.

The instant the door closed behind him, she was out of the bed. How did she know she was any safer now than she'd been an hour ago? She didn't. That officer could have been the real deal, or not. But she could not afford to lie there and take her chances. She wasn't safe here.

She wasn't safe anywhere.

The thought struck her like a punch in the gut. She wasn't safe. And neither was Mikey and Leah.

What if Leah had tried to contact her? The only place Leah would know to go to find her would be back at her house. Sure, she always left her contact information hanging on the refrigerator in case Leah needed her, but she had no idea if Leah knew the number. Her imagination started working overtime with images of Leah sneaking back into her house and being found by Hudson.

No. She couldn't remain here. That was certain. She needed to go home. And if Leah hadn't shown up there, then Elise would make plans to find them. Should she call Ryan? He'd left his card on her bedside table. She snatched it up. Once she got home, she decided. If she called him now, he'd probably tell her to stay in the hospital and let the police take care of it.

Good advice, except the hospital had already proved to be dangerous for her health.

Fearing someone would come in, she hurried to get dressed. Fortunately, she didn't need to worry about the IV any longer. She tied her shoes, then moved as soundlessly as she was able to the door and pulled it open just a teeny crack. Enough to let her slip out.

No one was there.

You'd think there'd be security. Then she heard voices and opened the door a tad bit wider. Ah. There *was* a security guard in the hall. And he was flirting with the cute night nurse at the desk. If she wasn't sneaking out, it would no doubt annoy her that the guard wasn't more vigilant. As it worked in her favor, though, she decided to take advantage. Slipping out the door, she moved quickly and turned down the next hall.

Within moments, she was striding out of the hospital and into the cool night air. Now what? Her car was back at her house. The buses wouldn't start their routes for another three hours. And there were no taxis waiting outside the hospital. She pulled her cell phone out of her purse. Dead. Of course. Maybe if she walked to the gas station on the next corner, someone would let her use their phone to call for a cab.

"Elise! Is that you?"

Startled, Elise whirled around. A woman had pulled her car up to the curb and rolled down the window. She'd recognize the black spiky hair anywhere. Angie Yates, the college student who used to watch Mikey. "Oh, hi, Angie. What are you doing out at this time in the morning?"

Angie raised her finely drawn eyebrows. "I was

about to ask you the same thing. I'm just heading back to the dorm after spending the weekend with my mom. You?"

Elise wrinkled her nose as she contemplated whether or not to tell her the truth. Angie was a bit of a rebel. She might enjoy aiding and abetting a fugitive. "Actually, I am making an escape from the hospital. I was in a bit of an accident earlier and they wanted me to stay overnight for observation. But I feel fine, so I am trying to make it home."

As she suspected, Angie's full lips widened into a grin, and her eyes lit up. "Girlfriend, let's get you home to your boy. Hop in."

Ignoring the ache in her chest at the reference to Mikey, Elise ran to the car and opened the door. She didn't attempt to explain the truth to Angie. She liked the woman, but they weren't close friends. She didn't have any of those. The less Angie knew, the better. The last thing she wanted was for Angie to decide the situation was too dangerous and change her mind about taking Elise home. The urgency to find Mikey grew with every moment that passed.

Angie kept up a steady stream of conversation as she drove to Elise's house. Elise's attention was scattered. She was grateful for once that Angie was happy with a monologue.

"Well, here we are." Angie shifted into Park and let the car idle in front of Elise's garage. Diana's car was gone. Someone must have towed it to the impound. Elise's car was still sitting partway down the driveway. "Why is your car all the way down there?"

"Oh, I came home earlier and stopped to check on something. That's all. I'll move it when it's light out."

"Why not get it now?"

"My car keys are inside the house."

"Can you get inside?"

"Yeah. I have a key hidden." And not in one of those easy-to-spot places like under a doormat, either. While Angie waited, she walked to the ornamental brick wall that started at the garage and lined one side of the driveway. It was about a foot tall. There was a loose brick butted up against the garage. Turning it slightly, she reached her hand in and pulled out the spare key. Angie waited until she was standing at the back door before she pulled back down the driveway.

That's when what she'd done fully registered.

She'd left the hospital where there was a security guard, even if he wasn't a very good one, to return to the place where she'd been attacked, and her baby-sitter had been killed. And she hadn't let the police know she was here.

Ryan wasn't going to be pleased with her.

She shook her head. Well, she was here now. And she very much doubted that Hudson had stuck around. He was after Mikey. She needed to beat him to it.

The house was quiet. Too quiet. A sob tore from her throat. Her poor baby wasn't here. Moving as if compelled, she soon found herself standing outside Mikey's room. Stepping into the doorway, her foot squished down on something. What? Reaching into the room, she flipped on the light switch. A second sob choked out of her. This time, though, it was a sob of fear.

Mikey's room had been torn apart. His toddler bed was on its side, the mattress sliced open. Her eyes flickered to the floor. She'd stepped on a stuffed rabbit. Or what had once been a rabbit. Bending down, she picked up the small animal. Mikey slept with that rabbit every night. The urge to be sick was strong. Covering her mouth with one hand, she squeezed her eyes shut and bent over at the waist. After a few minutes, the urge subsided, although she still felt queasy.

Ryan had said that the rest of the house had been relatively untouched. She knew he had.

One thought went through her mind.

She'd been wrong. Hudson had stuck around or come back.

What reason could Hudson have had to come back and trash his son's room? He had to have been looking for something. Something other than his son.

"Where is she?" Ryan glared at the young security officer and the night nurse. "Your patient, Miss St. Clair, is not in her room."

"Of course she is!" the security guard blustered.

His face reddened as he met Ryan's glare. He broke eye contact first. Probably because he'd been caught neglecting his duty. Ryan had no patience for people who'd sworn to serve and protect and took that obligation lightly. He couldn't remember the last time he'd been this angry. Or this scared. Elise St. Clair, who'd been little more than a husky voice on the dispatch radio for so long, was now a pretty woman with a missing nephew and who was herself in grave danger. And he had begun to care. That's what happened when you suddenly saw someone as a real person. His gut clenched just knowing that she was out there on her own somewhere in the wee hours of the morning with a killer after her.

When he'd woken up to find a text from Officer McLachlan notifying him that Elise had been attacked at the hospital and Security had been notified, Ryan had found himself dressed and heading to the hospital without a thought about the time or what he would do when he arrived. Part of him had been embarrassed rushing up to her room like a rookie. The moment he'd seen the state of affairs, though, he had thanked God for guiding him to where he was needed.

"No, she's not there," he informed them. "I was just in her room. Her clothes are gone, as are her shoes. When did you last see her?"

The guard started to splutter off an excuse. Ryan's cell pinged. He looked at the screen and let out a sound that was part sigh of relief and part grumble of frustration.

Snuck out. At home.

"You two are fortunate. She just texted me. This is still going in my report. And I will be notifying your supervisors."

The two looked thoroughly chastised. He almost felt bad them. For the briefest second, he considered letting the matter drop. Then an image of Elise fighting an attacker invaded his mind. No, there was no excuse for leaving her unsupervised when they knew she was in danger. He'd told them her room needed to be watched when he'd left. She had almost died. Again. Fixing a glare on them, he waited long enough to be sure that his message wouldn't be forgotten before spinning on his heel and striding toward the elevator.

As the doors slid closed behind him, he allowed his chin to drop.

"Thank You, Jesus, that Elise is alive. Guard her, Lord. And help me not to mess this up."

The elevator hiccuped, and the doors whooshed open. Setting his jaw, he stalked out of the hospital. Once outside, the urge to hurry pushed him to a jog until he climbed into his cruiser. He notified the station that he was leaving his current location and heading to Elise's place.

As his vehicle wound up the lane that led to her house, Ryan was struck by how inconspicuous the place looked. No one would ever guess just by looking that someone had been killed here mere hours before. Or that Elise had nearly lost her own life. A shiver traveled up his spine. He was reminded of a similar scenario years before. His best friend Ricky's face flashed through his mind.

He shoved it away. He needed to focus. Elise was alive. Unlike Ricky. He'd been on time to save her, and would do everything in his power to protect her and find both Mikey and Leah. Being a police officer was more than a job to him. It was a sacred call. And it was his way to make sure that what had happened to Ricky wasn't meaningless.

He pulled up in front of the garage and turned off the engine. There were lights on in the house. Actually, it looked like Elise had turned on every light. Probably to make herself feel safer. Or to keep the house from feeling so empty without her child. He could only imagine how hard it was for her to be inside, knowing what had happened before and not knowing where her nephew was.

As he stepped out of his car, his cell phone rang.

He glanced at the screen. It was Elise. He clicked it to accept the call.

"Elise?"

"Ryan?" Her voice was hushed. Why was she whispering? She sounded freaked-out. "I hope you just pulled in."

Ah. It made sense that she'd be worried when she'd heard the car approach.

"Yeah. I'm on my way in."

"I'll meet you by the back door. You need to see something."

The phone clicked. She'd hung up. He shrugged and sauntered to the house, keeping his eyes peeled for any sign of movement. Everything looked in order, but the hairs on the back of his neck stood on end.

Never one to ignore his instincts, he called Jackson, knowing that he'd just be coming on duty.

"Hey, Parker. What do ya know?" Jackson answered with his usual greeting.

"Not much," he replied drily. "Listen, I'm at Elise's house. She has something she needs me to see. I got the sense she's this close to freaking out." He glanced around again. "And I can't shake the feeling that something's off. You busy?"

"Nah, just paperwork. I'll come out."

Satisfied, Ryan disconnected. It was always better to have backup. He'd learned that early on. And he had the bullet scar to prove it. Ruefully, he rubbed his side where the bullet had exited. The old injury didn't bother him, not anymore. But on nights like this, it was a reminder of how fragile life was.

As if he needed that. He'd learned all about the fragility of life at the age of sixteen. That lesson had driven him to reject his father's dreams of his becoming a doctor like his parents and become a police officer, instead. A path that his father still didn't approve of.

Ryan shook off his reverie and met Elise at the back door. Even scared, she was just about the prettiest woman he'd ever seen. Her short curls brushed her jaw, making his hands itch to reach out and brush them back.

He held in a snort. Yeah, that would be appropriate. He was here for a purpose. And romance wasn't it.

"You said you had something I should see?" He winced. His voice had come out a little brusque. Something about her knocked him off balance. She set off all his protective instincts, and then some. Fortunately, she didn't seem to notice anything off in his tone. That was good, but at the same time, the fact that she didn't seem to be suffering from the same attraction he felt irked him.

Get over it, Parker.

"It's upstairs. Come on." Elise held the door open so he could enter. As he passed her, he caught a whiff of a light floral scent, so subtle it was barely there.

"Jackson's on the way. I'm going to tell him to text me when he gets here. Let's lock the door."

He sent the text while she slid the dead bolt into place, then followed her upstairs. She slowed as she neared a door on the right. The set of her shoulders tensed, and she drew in a deep breath before showing him the room. He whistled. It was obviously her bedroom, and it had been trashed. Drawers empty, the contents all over the floor. Her mattress thrown off the bed and sliced open. Closet open, the clothes strewn all over.

"Was it like this before?"

Ryan shook his head. "No. It had looked like a few things were out of place, but nothing was destroyed."

His phone pinged. He glanced down. "Jackson's here. I'm going to let him in."

Ryan hurried down to the back door, unwilling to leave her for long. He unlocked the door and swung it open. "Hey, Jackson. Come on."

Jackson raised an eyebrow. Ryan relocked the door, then lead the way back upstairs. Their uniform shoes made loud clomping noises on the hardwood of the stairs. Elise would know they were on their way back.

Soon the three of them stood side by side. Jackson's eyes widened, then narrowed as he surveyed the room.

"Why don't the bad guys just search without making a mess? They're just letting us know that they're out there. Seems it'd be smarter to search without giving us a heads-up."

Silently Ryan agreed, although he winced as he caught Elise's tormented expression.

"There's more."

Elise's voice was soft, broken. How much could one woman take? Ryan caught her hand and squeezed it, then let it go before she could comment. His ears were hot. Why had he done that? But he knew why. He hated seeing her in pain.

Without a word, she turned and led them to another room. It hardly seemed possible, but this one was wrecked even worse than the first room. And Parker had to agree with Elise. Whoever had done this wanted her to see it.

"Is he trying to scare me?" she whispered. "Because it's working. I'm terrified."

FIVE

The hard heels of the police-issue shoes worn by both officers echoed in the open room as they crossed the hardwood floors. It was almost like she was standing on the field with the marching band again during the halftime show in high school. There'd been many nights where she'd left the field with her ears ringing from all the noise. Still, right now she found the sound comforting. She closed her eyes and leaned her head back against the hallway wall as the men went over the scene. She had stepped out of the room as soon as they had put on their disposable gloves and activated their body cameras.

Her tired brain was trying to process everything that had happened. She knew that other cops would arrive soon. Her home was once again a crime scene.

Her eyes popped open. Her home was a crime scene.

And she'd contaminated it. How could she have been so stupid? She was a 911 dispatcher. She knew better. And yet she had walked right into that mess without a thought before she'd called Ryan. She'd even picked up that rabbit. As much as she didn't want to, he'd have to be told.

It was now completely daylight. The long night was catching up with her. All she wanted to do right now was to curl up on the floor, fall asleep and wake up to find it was all a horrible dream. Unfortunately, it wasn't a dream. And if she ever doubted it, she had enough pains and bruises for proof.

She couldn't wait any longer. Stepping into the doorway, she watched the two men working so seriously in the mess. She winced as she looked into the chaos. If possible, it appeared even worse in the daylight.

She really didn't want to say what she needed to say. Well, Elise wasn't a coward. She straightened her shoulders and took a deep breath to brace herself.

"Hey, guys?" She grimaced as both officers immediately turned to face her. Better just get it over with. "I'm afraid that I've already contaminated the scene." She dropped her eyes, not wanting to see their disbelief. "I know, I know. I've been working as a dispatcher and alongside the police long enough that I know better. But when I saw the mess, I kind of freaked out. That's my only excuse. All I could think of was that somebody was in Mikey's room. Violating my house and destroying my nephew's things. Sorry."

Elise blinked. Her eyes blurred anyway. She'd really messed up. What if she had damaged a clue that could have led to finding Mikey? How would she live with herself? She rubbed her chest as if she could soothe the pain away.

A hand on her shoulder startled her. Flinching slightly, she looked up to meet Ryan's concerned brown eyes. She saw no condemnation, only compassion. The urge to move forward just an inch or two so she could lay her head on his shoulder nearly overwhelmed her. She was so sick of having to always be strong. Instead, she gave him a weak smile and backed up a step.

His arm dropped back down.

Had she hurt his feelings? His expression gave nothing away. She was most likely overreacting. Again. Seemed she was doing that a lot lately.

"Elise, you're human. We've all messed up crime scenes before. Sometimes you just can't help it. It happens."

Yes. It happened. She wasn't naive. She knew that there were always circumstances out of one's control.

It was hard to be nonchalant, though, when the lives of innocent people were at risk.

Jackson was muttering to himself, shaking his head.

"What are you thinking, Jackson?" Ryan turned away from her, his gaze shifting as it moved over the destruction again. Even if she'd never met him, she would have known he was cop. It was in the way he held himself and in the way his gaze never stopped moving, constantly on the lookout for danger.

"This doesn't make sense, Parker. The timeline is weird."

Ryan tilted his head, furrows digging into his brow. Slowly he nodded. "I see what you mean. It does seem odd. And the motivation is off, too."

Frustration bit at Elise. "What's off? What are you talking about?" It seemed to her that anytime someone targeted a child something was wrong. But wrong or not, it still happened. So what made this case different?

"You were attacked at the hospital, right? So someone wants you dead."

"Yes. Hudson. I told you, he blames me for his problems." Her shoes made staccato sounds as she tapped her feet.

"And probably because you can identify him," Jackson offered.

What were they getting at? She already knew that Hudson had it in for her. He'd said as much before he tried to strangle her. Sending someone after her in the hospital had been added confirmation that he wanted her dead. As if she needed any more proof.

"Elise." This time she didn't step away from Ryan as he put a hand on her arm. "The man who attacked you at the hospital wouldn't have had enough time to come here and cause this much destruction. And I know for a fact that the crew who took over for Jackson and me were here for several hours after we left. They were told to photograph and search every nook and cranny of your house."

She shook her head, confused.

"I would add that the destruction we see here seems at odds with the manner of the previous search," Jackson threw in.

Lord, what's happening here? I'm lost.

The hand on her arm tightened, the thumb rubbing in comforting circles. She wasn't alone. God was with her. And He had sent her protection in the form of these two officers.

She tried to speak. Had to clear her throat to loosen it. "What are you telling me?"

It was probably going to be bad news and she didn't want to know, she really didn't. Unfortunately, she needed all the information possible if she was going to survive long enough to see Mikey and Leah safely returned.

"What we're saying is that it looks like Hudson isn't the only one after you."

Her world fell apart completely. Stumbling back, she bumped into the wall. It was good it was there. Otherwise, she just might have wilted into a dejected puddle of grief in the middle of the hall.

Strong arms reached out and gave a gentle tug. Elise didn't resist as she was drawn forward. She was so tired of being strong. All the sorrow of the past three years, as well as the fear from the current situation, welled up and wouldn't be held back. Giving in, she buried her face in Ryan's shoulder and gave in, allowing the tears to flow from her very soul in a cathartic rush.

He'd never had a woman cry in his arms before. It wasn't a comfortable feeling. In fact, it was awful. Every sob caught at his heart, making him feel helpless.

This had to be a new record. The same house being attacked twice in under twenty-four hours. If he had any doubt about whether or not he needed to move Elise to a new location, it was erased now. There was no way anyone could stay here under these circumstances.

Unfortunately, he had the feeling she wasn't going to be cooperative.

And he was right.

The second he started talking about her packing a bag and getting ready to go to somewhere else, for even just a few days, she crossed her arms and glared at him so fiercely he would not have been surprised had she decided to take a swing at him.

He didn't blame her. Not really. She wanted the comfort of her own home after her whole life had been turned upside down. And from what she'd told him earlier, it wasn't for the first time.

But while he didn't want to be callous, he had a job to do. And his job would be made a whole lot easier if he could count on her being safe. That wasn't going to happen here. Not when Hudson Langor, or whoever else was involved, was so confident that he or they would break into her house *twice*. And if they'd do that, the odds were strong that they were to blame for the attack at the hospital.

It was hard to believe that even one person, let alone two, had a grudge against the stunning woman standing so close. Again, he thought about the attack in the hospital.

His stomach churned, but he didn't feel sick. No, instead, hot fury shot through his system. If she hadn't pulled the IV loose, the nurses wouldn't have known to go to her room. It was very likely that the lovely, angry woman in front of him would now be dead.

"How can I leave?" she demanded now. Under the hard, strident tone, he caught the subtle layer of anguish. That was a feeling he had too much personal experience with. He opened his mouth to respond, but she continued. "What if Leah comes back to look for me? Someone has to be here just in case she tries to contact me."

"Look, Elise, I get what you're saying. I really do. But the simple fact is people are out to get you. People who have already attacked you personally not once, but twice, in under a day. I don't think we can take any more chances. This house is not safe for you. I promise I will keep trying to find Mikey and Leah. We all will. They are a priority. But keeping you alive is also a priority."

She stepped closer to him and gripped his arms with her hands as she searched his face. He held still. Something in his face must have convinced her, for she sighed and nodded. The slumped set of her shoulders nearly tore him apart. It hurt to see her defeated. She'd been so strong up to now.

"Hey." He tapped her shoulder, willing her to look up. "Just because we're leaving doesn't mean we're giving up."

"I know." Her voice was just shy of a whisper. "But it feels so final. Still, I know that you're right."

If only there was some way to make her feel better. The only course of action available to him was to stop those who wanted to harm her, and to locate Mikey and Leah. He would do everything in his power to see that it happened. Even if it cost him.

A cruiser arrived with more officers to process the scene. Within an hour, they had finished with the crime scene. They uploaded the information from their body cameras and sent the files to the precinct. Ryan stepped into the kitchen to update the chief.

"What are your plans, Parker?" the chief asked.

Ryan swiveled to look out the window. His whole system was on high alert. Every movement he saw outside was a potential threat.

"Sir, Elise is definitely not safe here. We have no idea what we're dealing with. Jackson thinks there are multiple threats, and I agree. Elise has no idea who else, besides her brother-in-law, would be after her. I plan to set her up in the motel in town. I would like to request that she be kept under surveillance."

"That is a reasonable plan, Sergeant. Proceed and keep me up-to-date on the case."

"Yes, sir." Ryan disconnected the call and then went to find Elise and move out. He wouldn't rest easy until she was somewhere more secure.

As soon as her purple duffel bag was stowed in his trunk, they departed. Jackson gave a jaunty wave to him as he headed back to the station in his own cruiser. Unlike the day before, it was a warm sunny morning, the sky such a brilliant blue that Ryan was forced to don his sunglasses in order to see well enough to drive.

The drive started out silent. Ryan attempted to break the silence with small talk, but he was a hopeless failure at it. Besides, he really wasn't in the mood to talk, and Elise didn't seem to be, either. He liked to have quiet to sort out his thoughts and to process all that had happened. And he always did his best thinking in the car. Something about the majestic Pennsylvania landscapes helped him focus on whatever problem he was trying to work out. Which meant that he had trouble giving his attention to conversation.

Thankfully, Elise didn't seem to mind. She sat beside him, staring out the passenger-side window, her profile pensive. Every few minutes, she'd hum a melody, a poignant sound that didn't interfere with the reflective mood. Her voice was pleasant. Not fabulous, but restful. A voice meant for lullabies.

And again his thoughts were on Mikey. He said a brief prayer in his mind for the boy's safe return.

The silence was broken by a loud gurgling sound. Startled, Ryan jerked his head in Elise's direction.

Her face was flushed. One hand was pressed tight against her flat stomach. It didn't stop the second gurgle, louder than the first, from rumbling into the quiet. Ryan fought the grin that pulled at the corners of his mouth and lost. At least he managed to hold in the laugh that wanted to escape.

"I take it you didn't eat breakfast yet?"

Elise buried her face in her hands. Then she laughed. "It's pretty hard to deny it, with my stomach growling like that. How embarrassing."

He shrugged. "Nah. It happens."

Making a split-second decision, he pulled into a fast-food restaurant.

"What can I get you?"

Just for a moment, he thought she'd argue. Then she sighed and nodded. "I'm a vegetarian, so if I could get an egg-and-cheese muffin with no meat, that would be perfect."

He lifted an eyebrow in her direction. "I'm a carnivore. Does it bother you if I eat meat?"

She rolled her eyes. "Of course not. I just don't like it for myself."

He could live with that.

Fifteen minutes later, hunger satisfied, they pulled up to the motel where she'd be staying. The U-shaped motel was all one level, the doors opening into the parking lot. Not much of a deterrent to would-be killers, he reflected uneasily, although, the parking lot had security lights and cameras. And there would be a police officer stationed outside her room at all times.

"What about your job?" he asked. "Are you supposed to go in today?" Why hadn't he thought about that earlier?

Elise bit her lip. He had to look away for a moment. She was way too pretty for his peace of mind.

"I'm off today, but I'm scheduled for tomorrow. Should I call them?"

He debated with himself for a moment. If she went to work, it might help her to not dwell on the situation. And she should be safe enough there. "I think it would be okay for you to go back to work. But you need to be willing to call in at a moment's notice if something happens."

A grimace flashed across her face briefly. "I understand."

Well, there wasn't really more to be accomplished in the car. "Let's get you checked in."

He led the way to the office. The manager of the small motel was very cooperative. Although he didn't like the idea of a cruiser in his parking lot 24/7, he understood the need for it and agreed. Ryan signed Elise in under the name Emily Johnson.

"If anyone other than the police asks about a guest who resembles Ms. Johnson, you need to call me right away. And don't give away any information. Are we clear?"

By now, the man's eyes were starting to bug out of his head and his skin had gone a bit pale. No doubt he was wondering what kind of danger he'd brought upon himself. Nevertheless, he agreed to Ryan's terms. Ryan helped Elise get situated in her room. Then he hung out with her until his replacement arrived.

When he saw Lieutenant Willis pull in, he sighed, some of his tension leaving. Dan Willis was a rock-steady cop, one who took his job—and the protection of civilians—very seriously.

"My replacement is here. I will be back tomorrow. And in the meantime, I will let you know if I find out anything."

The woman before him looked suddenly lost. It made his chest ache. And that's when it hit him. He didn't want to leave her. He had a million things to do: calls to make, people to interview, reports to complete. None of that changed the fact that all he wanted to do was stay and protect her.

He had to be nuts. No way was he in any position to get so invested in her personally. Not only did he still need to build up his career to finally prove his calling to his father, but he had to find Mikey and Leah. He knew that Elise was merely surviving until that happened.

Still, he couldn't leave her looking so forlorn. Walking to her, he gently took her upper arms in his hands.

"Elise, I will keep looking. You know I will."

When she moved forward and wrapped her arms around him and laid her head on his shoulder, he was startled. But he realized she needed comfort. *This is not romantic, Parker.*

It sure felt that way.

He hugged her briefly, then released her. Bidding her to lock the door behind her and keep the drapes closed, he left.

Determination settled over him. She'd been attacked twice now. It was only a matter of time before another attack was attempted. Hopefully, whoever was looking for her wouldn't find her, but he knew he couldn't count on that. He needed to be ready. Because she depended on him, and he wouldn't let her down. No matter who was coming to get her.

SIX

The next day was not starting out as he'd hoped it would.

Ryan popped open a can of Pepsi and took a long swallow, hoping that the sugar and caffeine would give his tired body a boost. After a frustrating day with minimal progress, he'd tossed and turned last night, unable to shut off thoughts of Elise and her situation. Even when he'd drifted into a restless sleep, she'd been featured in his dreams, always running from some unknown enemy while he ran to catch up.

It was horrific. And he was paying for his restless night now. A yawn caught him off guard. He shook his head, then drained the rest of the can before tossing it basketball-style into the recycling bin against the wall.

"Two points." Lieutenant Jace Tucker stopped at his desk. "Are you coming down with something? Lookin' a little rough today, man."

Rubbing his hands down his face, Ryan muffled a snort. That was putting it mildly. "I'll cope. Hoping for a caffeine rush." He jerked his head in the direction of the recycling bin.

"Yeah, I can see that. You know, coffee would be a better stimulant."

Ryan shuddered in response. "Dreadful stuff."

Jace chuckled. "It is the way you make it."

"Then it's a good thing I don't have to taste it, isn't it?" It was the department joke that Ryan's coffee was comparable to motor oil. He didn't usually make it, but he knew that some of the other officers, most notably Chief Kennedy, enjoyed the foul drink. So if he was the only one available, he made it on occasion. But he refused to drink it.

"Any good news on the St. Clair case yet?" Jace unwrapped a stick of cinnamon-flavored gum, then offered the pack to Ryan.

"No, thanks." Ryan turned down the gum, then focused on the question at hand. "No real progress yet. No one has seen the girl or the child, and the picture of Langor hasn't had any hits, either." His voice had an edge. No doubt Jace had caught it.

"What about the Amish girl's family?"

Ryan was already shaking his head. "Sergeant Thompson visited them yesterday. They haven't seen Leah since she disappeared two days ago. I plan on stopping by today to check back."

Two hours later, he was standing at the door of the home of Leah's cousin Ivan Byler. Ivan was pleasant, but it wasn't hard to see that he was feeling uncomfortable. And that he wasn't pleased to have an officer at his house. Again. Ryan had the feeling that if it wasn't for the fact that his cousin was in danger, he would have politely asked the police to leave him be.

"Leah ain't been here since she left, like I said."

"I'm sorry to keep bothering you, Mr. Byler. We're

just trying to find everyone and get them home safe and sound."

"*Jah*, I understand. I want Leah home. She's a *gut* girl and helps my wife. Our fathers were brothers, before hers was killed last year in an accident."

Ryan filed that bit of information away, just in case it became important later on.

The Amish man hesitated. Something was on his mind. Ryan didn't push, but it was hard. Finally, Ivan nodded to himself. "Another Englischer was here. Yesterday, while my family was eating, asking about Leah, too."

Ryan's tension shot up another notch. Who else would be looking for her except those who wanted to harm Elise? Leaning forward, he said, "Can you tell me about this man? Please, it could literally mean life or death."

The man paled slightly, his eyes widening, but he answered. "*Jah*, his face was—" he made a motion with his hands, as if he was searching for the correct word "—damaged?"

"As if he'd been in a fire?" Ryan held his breath.

The other man thought for a moment, then nodded. "*Jah*, maybe so. He had a hand-sketched picture of Leah, drawn with pencil. My name was written on the side."

At those words, Ryan's blood ran cold. The image he'd scanned had gone out to precincts, but Elise had kept the original. So how had he gotten it? If Elise had taken it to the motel with her—

Urgency pounded through his veins. Elise needed him. Thanking Ivan for his time, Ryan ran back to his cruiser. He was still half an hour from Elise. He checked the time and relaxed slightly. She should still be at work. Although it couldn't hurt...

Punching the button for the phone, he barked, "Call the station," then drummed his fingers on the steering wheel while the phone rang.

When the receptionist picked up, he asked to speak with Chief Kennedy. A few seconds later, the chief's familiar drawl came on the line.

"Chief Kennedy here."

"Chief, it's Parker here. I have a bit of a situation." Succinctly, he informed the chief of his conversation with Ivan Byler. "I am on my way back to LaMar Pond. I can't make it in time to meet Elise as she gets off work, and I'm not comfortable letting her walk out without an officer there."

"I concur. Listen, Parker, I will send someone to escort her back to her motel. Then you can meet them there."

Disconnecting, Ryan felt a little better. Not completely. Though he would trust his fellow officers with his life, he needed to see Elise for himself. An image of her popped into his brain. Her brown curls with their honey-gold highlights, her wide hazel eyes that sparkled yet always seemed to be sad. And that sadness was from more than Mikey being missing. He'd noticed the first time that he'd seen her how sad they were. He would give much to see those eyes sparkle with joy instead.

Well, now she was depending on him, for herself and her nephew. If there was ever a case where failure wasn't an option, this was it. Even if he didn't sleep until she was reunited with Mikey, it seemed like a small price to pay to see her happy.

The drive back to LaMar Pond had never seemed so long. Not only did he get behind a slow, chugging farm machine, but he couldn't pass it for miles. Not when they were on the winding, hilly roads where one could never see far enough ahead to tell if there were oncoming vehicles. Maybe if there had been oncoming traffic, he might have at least felt better. But they didn't pass a single moving vehicle. Finally, the machine turned into a field. Without hesitation, Ryan pressed his foot down on the gas and sped up. And then he hit LaMar Pond. And proceeded to catch the red lights. Every. Single. One.

His jaw hurt from clenching it by the time he finally arrived at the motel. To his relief, Elise was there. She was waiting in her room with Sergeant Claire Zerosky, fondly called Sergeant Zee by her colleagues.

"Hey, Parker. Good to see you. I didn't think you were coming, you took so long to get here." Zee flashed him a teasing grin as she passed him. He rolled his eyes, but he could feel his ears grow warm. He looked at the clock. He'd actually made really good time. Even with the farm machine he'd trailed. Fortunately, she didn't ask how fast he went, because he'd gone plenty fast once he was able to. "I gotta go," Zee said. "It was nice talking to you, Elise."

"Same goes, Claire."

"Once things have settled down, let's do lunch."

"Absolutely. Let's."

Zee closed the door behind as she let herself out. Ryan turned to Elise with raised eyebrows. She shrugged in response. "Claire and I have been friends since I moved here." She tilted her head. "So why did

I need the escort today? I thought that someone would meet me here."

He drew in a deep breath, hoping she wouldn't freak out on him. Not that he'd blame her if she did. There was only so much one person could take. "Elise, I visited Ivan Byler today. He's Leah's cousin."

"Yes." She drew the word out, narrowing those gorgeous eyes slightly, making him think of a cat.

"He described a man matching Hudson's description coming around and asking after Leah." Those eyes widened. Her mouth fell open. He hurried on. "He said the man had a hand-drawn image of Leah."

"The picture Rebecca drew!"

"Exactly. Did you bring that picture with you?"

He hoped she'd say no. If she said no, then that would mean this man hadn't been in her motel room.

She bit her lip as she pondered the question. "I don't remember packing it. In fact, the last time I saw it, it was lying on the kitchen counter. I set it there when I got home, and forgot about it, what with everything else that happened."

It made sense to him.

"That means that Hudson had to have gone into your house after we'd left for here." He stepped closer to her. "Elise, he knows what Leah looks like."

She spun and stalked away, before spinning to face him again. She wasn't mad at him, he knew that. Still, her hazel gaze sparked with anger as she glared at him. "Does he know where she was headed? Did Ivan say anything about my nephew?"

He held up his hands in an instinctive calming gesture. "No, but if he was looking for Leah, he had to have suspected that she had Mikey. The fact that he doesn't seem to know where Leah is headed is good. At least, we still have that in our favor."

"For now. But what happens when someone spots them?"

Ryan's silence unnerved her. She knew him well enough to know that he wouldn't patronize her by lying or trying to pretty up what was happening. Unlike her ex-fiancé, Ryan had shown her the respect of treating her like an equal.

Why was she thinking about Brady now? She'd pushed his memory out after the way he'd betrayed her. Gotten rid of all the pictures, all the memories. She wasn't about to go through that again. And here she was, once again relying on a man.

But this is different. This time it's for Mikey.

She wasn't fooling herself. She'd wanted to stay in his arms last night. It had been so long since anyone had comforted her, had held her just because she needed it. And it had helped. That short-lived hug had helped her to feel God's peace, even if only for a few brief moments. She could get used to that feeling.

If she let herself. Which she wouldn't. The emotional cost of trusting a man, of loving a man, had nearly destroyed her before. It wasn't worth the risk. As soon as she had Mikey back, she'd walk away from whatever hold Sergeant Ryan Parker was starting to have on her. In the meantime, she needed to keep her distance.

That was going to be difficult.

It was more than how handsome he was. She'd learned how good looks could cover up a host of bad qualities such as cruelty and secrecy, in Hudson's case. And bone selfishness. That was Brady's weakness. That and his need to climb the social ladder. And anyone who he deemed a hindrance, including his adoring fiancée, well, they were shoved out of the picture.

"Elise? Um…you okay?"

"What?" She shook herself free of her memories. "Yes, I'm good. I was just thinking about something. Nothing important."

The look he gave clearly said he wasn't buying it, but he didn't push. Part of her really wanted to tell him about Brady. Of course, she didn't. And just the fact that she wanted to let him know about her past told her she was getting in further than she should.

"So what should we do? About the picture, I mean."

Ryan frowned, deep furrows knitting into his forehead. "Well," he began, "I am thinking we should go back to your house and look around, to see if there are any other clues. Maybe Hudson left something behind. Something that will give us a hint of where he's staying."

She interrupted him. "Or maybe Leah did come back and leave me a note or something. If he was still looking for her yesterday, then I think we can assume he didn't find her. Which means she's still alive out there."

He nodded. She didn't like the look on his face.

"Ryan Parker, don't even think of leaving me here while you search. You don't know my house like I do. If there's anything different or out of place, I'd see it before you. You know I would." It sounded like a logical argument. It wasn't likely to hold water, though. Who took a civilian to a crime scene? But she couldn't stay here. She just couldn't. She'd crack if she had to sit here and wait, knowing that every minute her baby got farther and farther away. She knew that time was critical in missing-children cases. The one thought that kept her going was knowing that the kidnapper in this instance was trying to save her baby, not hurt him. But Leah was only sixteen years old. How much hope was there for a young teenager from a small Amish community to protect Mikey against seasoned criminals?

Ryan opened his mouth to respond. She knew before he said anything that he was going to deny her request. His phone rang before he could answer her, delaying the inevitable.

"Yeah, Thompson. What's up?" His frown grew deeper as he listened. Several times, his gaze flickered to her, concern flaring in their depths. "That's okay, buddy. Don't stress about it. I have the situation under control until you or someone else can take over."

He listened to whatever Thompson was saying for several more seconds. When he finally hung up, his face was perturbed. His mouth tightened. Whatever Thompson had said to him, it wasn't good.

"I'm not saying that your argument isn't a sound one. It has some merit, though I think the officers at the department have the experience to locate clues." She opened her mouth to argue, but he ignored her and continued talking. "That being said, Thompson was supposed to take over your protection so I could check the house, but there was another call that he needed to respond to. I am not leaving you here unguarded. It looks like you're getting your wish. I just hope I don't regret this decision."

She snapped her mouth closed so fast her teeth clicked. She wasn't about to argue when it might make him change his mind.

Instead, she went meekly with him to his car. He placed a warm hand on her elbow, his gaze continuously moving as they walked. Her elbow tingled where he held it. It was silly, but the tension shimmering between them made her a little breathless. She flicked her eyes up to his expressionless face. Was he feeling the connection?

It was hard to tell, but she didn't think so. At least, he didn't appear to be affected by her like she was by him. Annoyance zipped through her.

Stop it, she told herself. *You don't want him to be attracted to you. You and he have no future. Even if he did like you that way, it would never work. You know that you can't be any man's wife. Not with your flaws.*

Ryan opened the car door for her, still looking around. She thought he wasn't going to look at her at all. She was wrong. As she stood by the door, ready to enter the vehicle, his eyes snapped back and met hers. Her breath caught at the electricity that flared between them. For an instant, they were both caught, snared in the same web.

Then she broke the connection, folding herself into the passenger seat. She placed her hand over her heart, trying to slow it down.

When Ryan entered his side, she couldn't look at him.

"Alrighty, then. Let's go." She could hear the forced cheer in his voice. Huh. Apparently, he was going to ignore whatever had just passed between them. She was good with that. Which didn't explain why she felt so annoyed.

The ride back to her house was again silent. But this trip was different. She could feel the thick tension crackling between them. Her shoulders bunched up. Who knew what they'd find at her house? Or if anyone would be waiting for them.

As they drove up the lane, Elise clenched her fists, the nails digging into her palms. She startled when Ryan placed a warm hand on one of hers. Despite her earlier resolution to distance herself, she gripped his hand, accepting the comfort.

A minute later, he pulled up in front of the house and stopped.

They exited the vehicle. The walk up to the back door felt like she was walking a gauntlet. At any moment, she expected something to happen. It was eighty degrees outside, a perfect July afternoon, but she was shivering with apprehension. The hair on the back of her neck tingled. She couldn't see anyone or anything, but every fiber of her being was screaming that they were being watched.

SEVEN

Ahead of him, Elise's muscles were so taut he expected her to snap.

He casually moved her faster, pushing her through the doorway. Once they were inside, he instructed her to lock the dead bolts. After pulling out his service revolver, he quietly searched through the premises, opening every closet and looking through every nook to make sure they were the only ones there. Once he was convinced that no one else was inside, some of the tension melted and his nerves settled.

Back in the kitchen, he peered out the windows. The sun was making it hard to see. He lifted a hand and held it in front of him to shade his eyes and help him see better.

Wait a minute. What was that? Ryan squinted and eyed the area behind the house. His gut knotted and a chill flashed through him.

Something was in the trees. Drawing his service weapon again, he flipped on his body camera. "There's something in the trees," he told Elise. "I'm going to investigate."

"No!" Elise caught at his hand. "Ryan, what if you get hurt? Or worse."

Warmth spread through him at the concern in her rich voice. He leaned over and kissed her forehead. Those eyes that continued to draw him in widened. A pretty flush spread over her face. He carried on as if nothing had happened. "I have to go, Elise. We need to catch whoever is behind these attacks. You stay in the house."

He started to take a step, then stopped. If something dangerous was there, and if he was incapacitated, that would leave Elise vulnerable. He reached for his phone and called the station for backup. When he was assured that it was on the way, he eased himself away from Elise. "I'll be back. Lock the door behind me."

Despite the mutinous set to her mouth, he heard the bolt slide into place once he was outside. He started toward the trees. He had barely gone half the distance when his phone rang. It was Elise.

He answered, keeping his voice low. "Elise? What's wrong?"

"Ryan? Is that you outside?"

The tremble in her voice caught at him. Then he frowned. Why was she asking? She'd watched him go outside.

"You know I am. I'm almost to the tree line. Are you okay?" The sense of foreboding spiked as he heard her take a harsh breath.

"I can see a shadow through the blinds. Someone is standing on the other side of the house."

He froze. Then the adrenaline kicked in. He sprinted around the corner of the house. A young man wearing a leather motorcycle jacket was standing next to the window, a large hammer in his hand. His intent was clear. He was preparing to break the window to gain entry.

"Police! Hands in the air!"

The man dropped the hammer, spinning in shock. He didn't put his hands in the air. Instead, Ryan saw the man raise his arms straight out, at shoulder height. He knew what that meant. Ryan fired his gun as the man went for his own weapon. Missed. A loud crack came from behind him. There were two of them. Ryan dove to the ground as a second gunshot filled the air. A bullet whisked past him, slamming into the tree at his left.

Lying on his stomach on the wet grass, he aimed quickly at the assailant he could see and fired back.

The man in front of him shouted and crashed to the ground. He'd hit his target, but the man still held on to his gun, which meant that he was still a threat.

Feet were pounding up from behind him. The other shooter was coming to join in the fight. Ryan was in a pickle. He had two armed men coming at him, one from each side. Sweat broke out on his brow. Scooting back so he had a view of both men, he didn't know how he'd get out of this one and still save Elise. He recognized the men facing him. Boys, really. Neither of them was more than twenty. They were both gang members wanted for several hits. Word on the street was that they took jobs for money.

Elise. If someone had put a contract out on her, she wouldn't be truly safe until those gunning for her were caught. All of them.

He prayed she'd stay away from the windows. If

he didn't make it, she'd be targeted next. Raising his gun, he tried to get both assailants in his line of sight. It was a useless effort, and he knew it. He was only one against two. And he only had one weapon. But he wouldn't go down without giving his best. The first man made a move to raise his own gun again. Ryan squeezed the trigger, his hands jerking slightly as the gun kicked back. This time the man abandoned his gun and let it fall, grabbing his upper arm and swearing. The second man came closer, and Ryan held the gun on him. Why hadn't that man shot again? Not that he was complaining, but it didn't make sense.

Until he saw the man trying to fire. Nothing. The gun was jammed. Ryan jumped back to his feet, keeping his eyes on both men.

He might make it out of this crisis alive, after all.

A siren split the air. Ryan could see the strobe effect as the red-and-blue lights rushed closer. Without delay, the assailant standing before him bolted, abandoning his wounded partner and heading for the trees.

A cruiser screeched to a halt. It was the most beautiful sound he'd ever heard. Jackson jumped out, leaving the motor running. "Police! Halt!"

He took off on foot after the fleeing man. Ryan took care of the injured man still moaning and muttering on the grass. Within two minutes, the injured man was completely subdued, his weapon safely confiscated. The other one had dashed out of reach, jumping into a car and zooming off, leaving his comrade to fend for himself. The remaining youth stared after where his partner had been, glaring, his eyes filled with hatred. Chances are that it wouldn't go well for his partner if they ever met up again. Not that that was likely to happen. The young man they had in custody was looking at spending the rest of his life behind bars.

Ryan rolled the man on his stomach and tugged his arms behind him, reciting the Miranda rights as he clicked the handcuffs shut.

"You okay, Parker?"

Jackson helped him pull the prisoner to his feet, but his eyes carefully surveyed his friend.

"Yeah. I'm good. I want to check on Elise, though. She's in the house."

Jackson nodded. "Safest place for her to be."

Ryan nodded without responding. He wouldn't be able to relax until he saw for himself that she was okay. And chances were good he wouldn't relax even then. Not while she remained at risk and her nephew remained missing.

Jackson shoved the prisoner into the police car. "There's no way I'm gonna bring this guy into the station. Not with the other one still running loose out there. You need backup."

"Better call for another car to come get him."

Jackson nodded. He stepped away from the vehicle so that the prisoner wouldn't overhear the conversation and made the call. Ryan stood by listening, lightly pounding his fist against his thigh as he waited.

Jackson pressed the end button, then cast him a sardonic smile. "You feeling antsy, Parker?"

"Huh?" Oh. He was acting restless. Forcing himself to still his fist, he straightened. "Ha-ha. No, I'm fine. Just thinking about the case." He made sure they were far enough away from the prisoner before he brought Jackson up to speed. "Hudson Langor apparently broke into the house yesterday and found the picture that Rebecca had drawn of Leah. He went to Leah's cousin's house asking about her."

Jackson whistled and then glanced at the criminal sitting in the back of his car. "We were obviously right about more than one person being after Elise. Are they working with Langor, do ya think?"

"Not a clue. We should know soon enough."

Ryan looked his colleague and friend square in the eyes. Jackson's blue eyes were glacier cold. Just like Ryan, he knew they were against a ticking clock. The Amber Alert has produced no leads so far. Not to mention the fact that so many people were gunning for Elise. But why? Did it all stem from her confrontation with her brother-in-law? Or was she mixed up in something even darker, something she hadn't told him about? Maybe something she didn't even fully understand herself? People got in over their heads all the time and then were ashamed to admit it.

As much as he hated to think about it, he knew he needed to keep his guard up around her. He couldn't trust her absolutely. Not when he still needed to prove himself as a cop.

No one else was going to die because he was distracted by a pretty face.

A wide beam of light startled him out of his reverie. The hum of an engine thrummed up the driveway. Both Ryan and Jackson tensed, their hands going to the service weapons securely attached to their belts. They relaxed as Officer Gabe McLachlan parked behind Jackson's cruiser. He and Officer Lily Shepherd exited the vehicle. "Hey, y'all," Mac called. "Chief sent us to get your prisoner."

"Aren't you guys off duty?" Ryan asked, even as he helped Jackson transfer the snarling, swearing killer to the other car. Shepherd and Mac were the newbies on the roster. Which meant that they often got stuck with the third shift.

"We will be soon. Had a late-night incident. Just getting back."

"Gotcha."

Transfer complete, they watched as Mac managed to turn the vehicle around in the wide drive, only going into the grass once. Pretty impressive. Of course, he had done a short-lived stint as a race car driver.

"Should we go see how Elise is faring?" Jackson broke the silence.

"Yeah." He looked back to where Mac and Shepherd had recently disappeared. "I'm glad to have you here as backup, but if this is a contract hit, it might be more than our department is prepared to handle."

The two men looked at each other. Ryan saw the grim expression settle on Jackson's face. He felt the same way. The chances of ending this case without further bloodshed were slim. And it was impossible to know who would strike next—and where.

Elise sat on the floor in the kitchen, her arms wrapped around her knees as she leaned back against the cupboard. The gunshots had ceased, but her legs still felt too shaky for her to stand. She couldn't believe herself. She was a trained 911 dispatcher. She knew what to do in a crisis situation. But all her knowledge had meant nothing when she realized that Ryan was out there being shot at. Shot by people who were coming to get to her. And because of her, that strong, sweet, brave man was putting his life in danger. The final straw had been listening to the silence after all the shots had ceased. Her mind had started to play tricks on her. Maybe Ryan had been hit! Maybe he was even then trying to get to the house.

It was when she realized that her hand was on the dead bolt that she came to her senses. Was she really planning on stepping outside to check on him? Doing that might distract him and put him in even more jeopardy. She had backed away and stumbled against the cupboards, where she had stayed ever since.

The stress from the past three days was taking its toll. She allowed her head to loll to the side and closed her eyes. Weariness pressed down on her. It felt like she had lead weights over her shoulders. Where was her baby? And Leah? She hadn't really known the girl that well, but she certainly didn't deserve to be put in danger, especially since she had placed herself at risk to protect Mikey. She whispered a prayer for the teenager she'd hired to clean her house.

Someone knocked on the kitchen door. She jumped. Her heart stopped as the blood roared in her ears.

"Elise? Elise—open the door. It's me—Ryan. And Jackson's here, too."

Scrambling to her feet, Elise rushed to the door, tripping over her own feet. Her fingers trembled as she undid the main bolt and slid the safety chain back. It seemed to take her forever to open the door. When she did finally open it, it was all she could do not to throw herself into Ryan's arms. He represented all that was safe in her world right now. She restrained the impulse. Wouldn't that be a great way to embarrass both of them?

"Did you get him? Was it Hudson? Are you okay?" The questions tumbled off her lips one after the other. As she sucked in a breath she noticed that both Parker and Jackson had amused grins on their faces. Suddenly she felt defensive and lifted her chin. "What?" A soft chuckle rolled out of Ryan. As the smooth sound rolled over her frayed nerves, she shivered. And chastised herself for it. She didn't have time for this.

"I wasn't sure you were going to give me time to answer any of those questions."

Heat crawled up her face. It had been a long time since she'd been this rattled. There was a reason for it, that was true. But, deep inside, she hated the fact that Ryan was the person who was seeing her acting this way.

The smile slipped off Ryan Parker's face as quickly as it had appeared. Suddenly the man standing in front of her was all cop, searching for a killer. And for her nephew, the one bright spot in her life.

No, that wasn't true. No matter what happened she always had God's light with her. She'd not been as faithful as she should have been in the past few years, allowing other people, other situations, to come before her relationship with God. Right now, though, she knew that she needed Him to help her to overcome and survive. No matter what happened, she couldn't allow herself to put God on the shelf again, talking to Him only when she needed Him. He deserved better from her.

"Elise…" Ryan's voice broke through her reverie. She shivered at the intensity in it. "This is gonna be hard for you to hear, but it's important. The two guys that were out there—"

"Two?" she squeaked.

Those chocolate-brown eyes softened. "I'm sorry, Elise. But, yes, there were two men out there with guns. I recognized both of them. If I had to guess, I would say that they were contracted to kill someone."

He didn't say, but she understood his message. "Someone put a hit out on me?" Her ears buzzed. A wave of light-headedness hit her. She barely noticed the strong arms that swept her up and carried her to the front room before everything went black.

When she came to again, she was lying on the sofa, with a fleece throw tucked over her. That almost made her laugh. It was eighty degrees outside, and she was sweating under a fleece blanket. All laughter fled when she noticed the two worried police sergeants standing over her.

"I'm okay." She sat up. Ryan moved forward to help her, but she waved him back. "Seriously, Ryan. I'm good now."

He didn't look convinced, but he backed up, letting her have her space. She needed to take charge of herself. If she didn't, he wouldn't want to keep her in the loop. And she needed to be a part of this investigation.

"Okay," she said. "So who do you think put the hit on me? Was it Hudson?"

Ignoring the glances that passed between the two officers, she waited it out. Surely they'd tell her something if she was patient and didn't let up.

Finally, Ryan nodded. "It might have been Langor. At the moment, that seems like our best guess. Your sister was correct. We've found evidence that Langor had some ties to a crime syndicate."

She drew in a breath, shocked. It was one thing

to have thought it, but quite another to have it confirmed. "Apparently, he was hired to do different jobs. Theft, money laundering. Murder. He was discreet and charismatic."

"Not to mention the little fact that he didn't seem to care what they hired him to do as long as it paid well," Jackson ground out, his voice filled with disgust.

Ryan nodded. "Yeah. That, too. In fact, I talked with the police department that had dealt with your sister's murder. After we informed them that he was still alive, they looked at his file again. They called twenty minutes ago. They believe that he was paid to kill her, too."

She'd known it. As frightening as it was to hear it from Ryan, she'd known that Hudson was capable of horrible deeds. And she'd never doubted that he was the one who'd murdered her sister. Nor, if she was honest with herself, did it surprise her that he'd been part of a crime group. Had there been any clues to his true nature when he'd first appeared in their lives? Or had he changed?

It was so long ago she could barely remember.

The couch sagged as Ryan sat down. Jackson left the room. "Elise, talk to me."

"My sister was all I had for so long, did you know that?"

He shook his head, his eyes never leaving her face. "It's true," she told him. "Our parents died when I was two. Karalynne was four years older than me. She was my protector. They placed us with a few different foster families, but it never took. When I was ten, we were adopted. To a family who wanted us only until they had kids of their own. Then we were a nuisance. As soon as I was eighteen, I moved out and stayed with Karalynne. When she got married, I found my own place, but we were always each other's best friend. Hudson tried to stop that. He deliberately set out to separate her from those she loved."

Her phone chimed. So did Ryan's. Within seconds, the dispatcher radio in her kitchen went off. She recognized Monica's voice.

Several departments were called out, including LaMar Pond. "Shots fired on Mountain Lodge Road. Multiple entrapment."

Jackson ran back into the room. He and Ryan stared at each other. Mountain Range Road wasn't that far from her house. It could have been a coincidence, but she didn't believe that. And, judging by their expressions, neither did Ryan or Sergeant Jackson. LaMar Pond was a small town. Two incidents involving guns in a single day was almost unheard-of.

Had Hudson struck again?

EIGHT

What else could possibly go wrong? Ryan didn't even want to pursue that line of thought. Too many things could go wrong. Without knowing how widespread the contract on Elise was—and he was pretty sure that's what they were dealing with—the threat had just multiplied. Exponentially.

"Are you going to take me back to that motel?" Elise asked. Her words were meek. Her tone was anything but. And why not? The idea of trying to keep her safe in that motel with a single door between her and the outside world was ludicrous. One patrol car stationed outside the door was not going to be enough to protect her, and they didn't have a large enough force to put much more manpower on the scene.

"Honestly, Elise, at this point, I have no idea what we're going to do."

She was spoiling for an argument. Having grown up with two sisters, he knew the signs. He also knew that she wasn't mad at him. Rather, she was upset at the current situation. Most likely, she felt she had no control. He got that, and still he wasn't going to argue with her.

It was almost a relief when his phone rang.

"Hold that thought." He lifted a finger to stall Elise. The sparks that shot from her eyes were almost hot enough to burn him.

Swiping a finger smoothly across the front of his phone to unlock it, he answered the call. "Parker here."

"Parker, it's…Mac."

Mac? It sure didn't sound like Mac. The voice on the other end was weak and harsh. Gasping. It sounded like he was having trouble breathing. Ryan's senses went on high alert.

"Mac? Buddy, you okay? What's wrong?" Out of the corner of his eye, he saw Jackson's body snap around in his direction before striding toward him.

"Tires shot out. Car flipped. On its roof. Lily's unconscious." Ryan straightened, his glance shooting to Jackson, whose expression was flat, although concern shimmered in his eyes. Lily Shepherd had come on board around Christmas, the same time as Mac. She was quiet with a sharp wit. An excellent cop and a genuinely kind person. She was one of them. And now she was hurt. Mac, too, though at least he was still conscious. Mac continued, his voice growing weaker with each word. "The prisoner…he's gone. Dead. Two guys. They shot him through the window."

"Did you get a look at them?"

Mac drew in a harsh breath. "They came at us on motorcycles. Helmets on. Never saw…faces. And when the car flipped… I blacked out. Didn't see where they went. Trouble breathing…"

Pulse racing, Ryan drew in a deep breath to calm himself. He was grateful that the shooters hadn't decided to finish off the police officers. He frowned. Grateful, but surprised. It seemed a little off that they hadn't taken the time. Unless they had another agenda. One that focused on the woman standing mere feet away from him. He tensed. Elise was still their main target. No matter how much she protested, they needed to move out. Now.

Mac coughed on the other end of the line, his labored breathing lingering.

"Mac, where are you? Did you radio in your condition? I didn't hear the siren go off."

"Just did—"

At that moment, the pagers and the dispatcher radio Elise had in the kitchen all went off. Ryan instinctively flicked his gaze back to Elise. The argument had drained from her face, leaving it paper white.

He ended his call to Mac, saying a quick prayer for the safety of his two colleagues. They were good officers, good friends.

"We're getting you outta here now," he said to Elise, deliberately keeping his voice brisk. He wasn't going to argue. Not anymore. This was too important.

A sigh huffed out when she nodded.

"Where are we going?"

That was a good question. The motel was, of course, out of the question.

He thought quickly. "For now, why don't we head back to the station? I need to update the chief. He might have some suggestions for where you can stay."

He had to give her credit. She didn't argue. Sure, her lips tightened up and her hazel glance narrowed, but she followed him with no further argument. Ryan appreciated her acceptance. Feeling that time was their enemy, he and Jackson moved quickly to get her to the front door, pausing there to look around warily, making sure the coast was clear.

"You go first," Jackson murmured, his face blank. "I'll be right behind you. And once we're both behind the wheels, I'll drive out first."

He shot Jackson a concerned glance. Others might not recognize it, but he had known Jackson long enough to know that when his face went blank, he was dealing with strong emotions. Something about this was deeply upsetting his friend. There was nothing he could do, though. He respected Jackson's privacy. And, anyway, now wasn't the time to press him to talk.

Nodding, Ryan got himself and Elise into the cruiser and waited for Jackson to back out first. At the road, Jackson waited for Ryan, allowing him to move onto the road without running the risk of another car coming in between them. Without hesitation, Ryan flipped on his lights as soon as he started forward. Jackson followed suit. They both held off on the sirens. The strobe lights from two police cars would be enough to keep most people out of the way.

It was almost six when he escorted Elise into Chief Kennedy's office. Her eyes cut to the side of the desk where the chief kept his prized possession: a picture of himself and his wife, Irene, on their wedding day. Standing with them were AJ and Matthew, Irene's sons, and the chief's beloved stepsons. Briefly, pain flared in Elise's eyes before she turned back to the chief, seating herself in the chair he offered her.

Ryan looked at his boss with concern. The chief's face was missing his usual grin. And no wonder. Two of his officers were on their way to the hospital. Paul Kennedy took the care of his officers very seriously. When Ryan been shot a year ago, his chief had been there for him. All the way. The chief took every case seriously, but when one of his officers got hurt, his drive to catch the people responsible got even stronger. Whoever these men were, they didn't know what trouble they'd brought on themselves.

"Miss St. Clair. I am sorry to hear about everything that has happened to you and your family. Please know we're doing all we can to locate your nephew. And in the meantime, we're committed to keeping you safe. I have heard that you're being put up at the motel."

"Yes, Chief Kennedy. But I'm not comfortable about going back now."

The chief nodded. "I believe I know most of the facts, but let's go over them again to make sure we have all the details covered."

Ryan placed a hand on her shoulder, hoping she'd get the hint to let him take over the explanation. He knew what to say to convey the full danger of the situation. She merely lifted her wide eyes to his, then she smiled and gave a slight nod. Almost like royalty, he thought.

The chief cleared his throat. Oh. Yeah. He was supposed to debrief his boss. Launching into an explanation to cover all the new developments in the case, Ryan watched for the chief's reaction.

"Hmm. Well, I have to agree with you about the motel not being safe, Parker. We'll find another option—though hopefully, you won't have to be there for long. I am going to reach out to the surrounding precincts to bring some more people in. The more boots on the ground, so to speak, the faster we'll be able to root out this syndicate and stop it at its source. At least that is my hope."

"Mine, too, Chief." Ryan allowed his hand to drift once more to Elise's shoulder. As much to reassure her as to prove to himself that she was still safe.

The warmth of Ryan's hand on her shoulder anchored her. She'd sat there, listening as he'd related to his chief all that had happened. His tone had been clipped, unemotional, but listening to the precise recitation had Elise reliving all the terrifying events again in her thoughts. As a result, Elise was ready to crawl out of her skin. She was a woman who was more comfortable with action. All this standing around was stretching her past her limits of how much she could endure.

Then Ryan had put his hand on her shoulder and her frayed edges had smoothed. Not completely, but enough for her to regain her composure.

The door burst open. She jumped, grabbing on to Ryan's hand in her anxiety. It was Miles Olsen, the officer she'd met in the hospital—Rebecca's husband. Elise huffed out a breath, then realized that she was still holding Ryan's hand. She made the attempt to let go. Only she couldn't. Because he was still holding on. She glared at him, trying to inconspicuously pull away. He squeezed her fingers in response, flashing her his heart-stopping grin, before releasing her hand. Her cheeks reddened when she realized that Chief Kennedy had caught the entire exchange. Fortunately, the man didn't say anything. Nor did he appear to be upset. In fact, she was sure he looked amused before turning to face the new arrival.

"Olsen?" His voice was calm.

"Chief!" Olsen exclaimed. "We got a hit on the Amber Alert put out on Michael St. Clair."

Her mouth was dry as Elise sat up straight.

"Where? When?" the chief barked out, all signs of amusement gone.

"In Grove City, sir. Or right outside there. An elderly couple gave an Amish girl and a little boy a ride yesterday."

"Grove City? Why would Leah be heading there?" Ryan broke in, confused.

"They didn't say—"

"She wasn't heading for Grove City," Elise interrupted. At once, she became the center of attention. She focused on Ryan. "Don't you remember? Rebecca said that Leah's from New Wilmington. She was heading home. Where she thought she could hide and keep my little boy safe." As soon as she said it, Elise knew she was right. New Wilmington was where they needed to go. And she had to convince all of these strong, dedicated men that she needed to go with them, instead of being hidden here in LaMar Pond.

"That's right." Ryan snapped his fingers. "Chief, I would like your permission to start out that way. Obviously, I'd reach out to the local precinct, but I really want to see if we can track down Leah and Mikey. Before—" He broke off.

Elise knew what he was going to say. "Before Mikey's father gets to them."

"Elise…" Ryan said. She got the impression that he wanted to comfort her but really didn't know how.

"I know, Ryan. And I thank you for wanting to spare me the harsh details. I really do. But this is my kiddo we're talking about. And whether I like it or not—and I most certainly don't like it—there are men out there who want to track my boy down, and who also seem to want me dead. I'm still not completely sure why. It feels surreal. But I can't ignore the facts."

Even though I want to, she thought. She was sure that the sentiment was understood by all.

As it turned out, she need not have worried.

The chief turned to Ryan. "Parker, I agree that you should go to New Wilmington. Immediately. We will keep Miss St. Clair—"

"Actually, Chief," Ryan interjected, his gaze locked squarely on his boss. "I know it's not usual, but I had planned on keeping Elise with me."

"Explain yourself." Chief Kennedy's voice was firm but not angry.

He was, Elise remembered, a reasonable man. For the moment, she was content to allow Ryan to plead her case. Hiding her away hadn't kept her safe, so there was no reason to think a new safe house would be any more secure. The best way to protect her was to keep an officer at her side—and if she was going to be sticking with Ryan, then it just made sense for her to help him follow up on this new lead in the search for Mikey.

If the chief wouldn't bend, however, she would have no qualms about speaking up. No one—and she meant no one—would keep her from looking for her baby.

She glanced at the clock. Ryan bumped gently against her. What? She followed his gaze. Oh. Her leg was bouncing impatiently, the heel of her boot making rapid clicking noises against the floor. With effort, she forced herself to sit still as she concentrated on the conversation.

Squeezing her shoulder in reassurance, Ryan turned to face his chief again. "We've agreed that Elise can't go back to the motel—that she needs more protection than that provides."

"Agreed," the chief said. "She needs all the protection we can offer. But bringing her on the search for the Amish girl and the little boy doesn't sound like protection—it sounds like putting her right in harm's way."

Ryan grimaced, and Elise tensed. Was the chief going to insist on her staying away from the search?

"It's like this, Chief," Ryan explained. "First, Elise is the one who is best able to recognize Leah and Mikey. Even with the sketch we have, none of us have ever seen Leah's full face. And you know the Amish dress so that none of them stand out. We might not spot her in a crowd. Then there's the fact that none of our pictures of Hudson Langor are accurate. Again, Elise is the only who knows him and his voice."

He stopped to take a deep breath. Then he spoke more quietly, as if to make what he was going to say less harsh. "And finally, sir, we have no clue how many people are after her. We still haven't figured out who is the boss of the crime syndicate that Hudson was hired by. Or why they have decided to make her a target. Clearly, they're serious, though, if they killed one of their own rather than allow him to go with the police." The chief nodded at this, and Elise began to grow hopeful. It seemed like he was beginning to be convinced.

Ryan then drove the point home. "She needs someone with her around the clock until these men have been caught. But we can't put all our resources toward solving this case *and* keep a guard on her all the time. Elise wants to be involved in the search. She has useful information to help, and she needs constant police protection. The best solution to keep her safe, find the child and close this case is to let her come with me."

Holding her breath, Elise waited to see what Chief Kennedy would say. He considered the facts slowly. She felt like a teakettle ready to come to full boil. So much frustration was building inside. Could none of these men feel the time getting away from them?

Finally, just when she was ready to scream and demand they act, Chief Kennedy nodded. "You make sense, Parker. I will let her go with you. Honestly, I don't know how we'd keep her safe here until those other precincts send us some help, not with you gone and two officers in the hospital."

Shadows passed over all three officers' faces. They were more than colleagues. They were family. More than what she'd had with Brady. She slammed the door shut on that thought. Brady was gone, and good riddance. He wasn't worth her time. Unwillingly, her gaze flew to Ryan. There was a man of strength and character. One who looked after those he cared about.

Whoa. Had she just put herself in that category? It didn't matter if her affection for him was growing. The two of them could never be. It would be selfish of her to allow herself to grow close to him.

"Any word on the injured, Chief?" She forced herself to listen to Ryan.

Chief Kennedy sighed. "They should make a full

recovery, but it'll take time—they're beaten up pretty badly. Lily is still unconscious, although they think her injuries aren't that serious. Mac, though, is going to be out for a while. A bullet pierced his lung. He's fortunate that he wasn't killed."

"I'm glad that they didn't kill them, but it doesn't make sense to me."

"Why did they kill their partner instead of taking him with them?" Elise blurted out the question before she thought about it. Was it rude of her to interrupt?

Neither man seemed upset, though, she was glad to note.

"I was thinking about that, Elise," Ryan replied. "The only thing I can think of is that they wouldn't have been able to get the back doors open to let him out. Not without breaking the windows, or forcing the door, or doing something else that might have taken too long, giving the officers a chance to catch them. I know it sounds horrible, but the fear of the man possibly spilling details to make a deal might have been more important than his life."

Chief Kennedy nodded. "That's as good a motive as I can think of. I don't really care why they didn't kill my officers. I'm just praising God that they didn't."

A shudder worked its way up Elise's spine. What kind of people were they dealing with, people who could kill someone they knew with no regret?

These were the same people who were coming to get her. The horror grew in her mind when she realized the full impact of the matter. They had been contracted to kill her. They would not hesitate or show an ounce of remorse. They would keep coming until she was dead.

NINE

"What on earth are they doing?" Elise leaned forward to gaze at the people who were lined up along the road, taking pictures of the bridge. Granted, it was a gorgeous covered bridge. The wood was white, and the top rose to a triangular point. From where she sat, she could see the beams crisscrossing inside. Functional, yet aesthetically pleasing.

"This is Banks Covered Bridge. It's famous. I don't know the whole story, but years ago, a popular television show filmed an episode here."

"Really?" That was interesting.

"Yep."

She studied at the bridge with renewed interest. "Ryan, look! Have you ever seen a buggy like that before?" The buggy was crossing the bridge, the horses' hooves echoing like thunder. The buggy itself had a light brown top, almost tan. All the buggies she'd seen back home had been black.

"New Wilmington is the only place you'll find 'em." Ryan pulled off to the side, allowing a couple of buggies to pass him. They were in his truck, rather than his cruiser, in order to blend in more. He'd also taken the time to change out of his uniform into faded blue jeans and a black T-shirt. He still looked like a cop to her. A gorgeous one, but a cop nonetheless. Especially with the gun sticking out of the back of his jeans. A flannel shirt was sitting on the seat between them. He'd taken it to wear over his T-shirt when they were out of the truck. He used the break in driving to check his phone. "It looks like I missed a call from the chief. Hold on a minute."

Watching the people clustered around the bridge, Elise felt the first tingle of unease creep up on her. She could see vehicles coming up behind them. They were sitting ducks while Ryan was checking the message. It was probably important, she knew that. She just hated being so out in the open.

Her mind drifted back to the Amber Alert. She'd checked her cell phone later, and she'd had a message regarding the sighting. Which meant that anyone with similar technology also had that information.

Including Hudson.

He could already be in New Wilmington. And what about the others who were after her and might target Mikey, as well? The truck cab suddenly felt like a cage. She couldn't help the whimper that escaped her. Her baby was so vulnerable!

"Hey. Hey, Elise. I'm right here. What's the matter?"

Without thinking about her resolution, Elise turned and grabbed at Ryan's arm. The muscles flexed beneath her fingers. "The Amber Alert! Ryan... Hudson might know where we're heading. He might already be in the area!" Her breath came out hard and fast, like she'd been running a marathon.

Covering her hand on his arm with one large hand,

he searched her face. That's when she knew. He had already thought of that. It was another reason he wanted her with him. To protect her and to help find her nephew. His next words confirmed her theory.

"I had thought of that. I didn't bring it up because I didn't want you to dwell on it. But, yes, it is possible that he knows where we are heading. I don't know that we have any choice, though. We have to do everything we can to locate your nephew."

"How could you not tell me?" A part of her felt betrayed.

"Tell you?" Ryan rolled his eyes. "Honey, you work for a dispatch center. I assumed that you would figure it out. It's part of the program."

For a moment, she was too thrown by the confusion caused by his casual endearment to respond. Ryan didn't strike her as a man who used words like *honey* loosely. She both dreaded and felt excited by this small insight into his thoughts. Ryan Parker was starting to care for her. She was sure of it.

Then, as her mind caught up with the rest of his words, she felt a little sheepish. Oh, yeah, she should have figured it out sooner. Her only excuse was that her mind and heart had both been absorbed in the drama that was her world at this moment.

Turning her head out the window to hide her burning cheeks, she watched a car maneuvering past them. The vehicle was far to the other side, allowing another buggy to pass. But instead of starting forward, the driver pushed his face close to the window, his narrowed gaze scrutinizing the Amish family in the passing buggy. Not just a curious scrutiny, either. He was searching for something. As his face turned more in their direction, Elise gasped and pulled back out of sight, sinking lower in her seat.

"That's him! That's Hudson!" She managed to squeeze the words from her tight throat.

Ryan jerked his head up and stared in the direction Elise had been facing.

Ryan moved to pull back onto the road, no doubt to chase Hudson. It was too late; Hudson had sped up and crossed the bridge the moment the Amish family had passed. Before Ryan could come onto the road, more vehicles had replaced Hudson's.

Among them were several motorcycles.

The riders were wearing T-shirts and vests. Only one was wearing a helmet. One of the men looked very familiar to her.

"Ryan, see that last guy?" she whispered, even though the windows were shut and the air-conditioning was on. She waited for his nod. "I had a problem with my power going out two weeks ago. He was the man who came out to fix it for me."

Ryan stiffened. "You sure of that?"

"Of course I'm sure!"

"Elise, that's the other guy who was at your house yesterday."

She could feel the blood draining from her head. "I let a contract killer into my house?" If she wasn't so freaked, she'd have been embarrassed at the squeak that left her mouth. As it was, she was afraid she was going to be sick on his leather seats.

He smoothed her curls tenderly back from her face. "You couldn't have known. But if my guess is right, he did more than fix your power."

She had no time to ask what he meant. He called

the chief. It surprised her that he put it on speaker. Then again, she'd hear his side of the conversation, anyway. The chief picked up immediately.

"Parker, did you get my message?"

That made her curious. She remembered that Ryan had said he'd had a voice mail.

"Yes, sir. But you should know, something more has happened. Elise saw Langor go across the Banks Covered Bridge. And not far behind him were three motorcycles, one of whom was ridden by the man I chased at her house. We have to assume all three are members of the gang after Elise."

"Did they notice you?"

Elise jumped when Ryan's hand caught hers. She'd been tapping her long nails against the dashboard. He didn't let go, just brought both hands to rest on the seat between them. With a sigh, she leaned back and closed her eyes while she listened.

"No, sir. But Elise recognized one as an electrician who visited her house."

A pause settled in the air before the chief, his voice thick with satisfaction, said, "So we're finally getting somewhere. If I were to guess, I'd say that her house is wiretapped or bugged."

"Agreed." Ryan squeezed her hand, no doubt to comfort her.

Her house was bugged. That creeped her out as much if not more than the fact that her room had been searched. How would she ever live in that house again? Even when she got Mikey back, to allow herself to live there...

She was getting ahead of herself.

The chief was speaking. "I will see that her house

is checked for bugs. As to Hudson being there, did you get a look at him yourself?"

"I did. I could pick him out in a crowd now."

After another minute, the call ended. Ryan twisted on the seat, moving so he was facing Elise. "Elise, the chief had called earlier because Lieutenant Tucker had learned the name of the man who put out the contract on you. Have you ever heard of a man named Leroy Dellon?"

Thinking, she shook her head slowly. "I don't believe so. Hold on." Fishing out her own phone, she flashed him a grin. "The internet knows everything."

So saying, she typed his name into a search engine and gasped at what appeared. The image of the handsome man that filled her phone was indeed familiar to her. "I can't believe it!"

"What? Have you met him?"

Turning the screen to Ryan, she said, her voice scarcely more than a harsh whisper, "This man owns the land directly next to mine. Two months ago, my neighbor died of a supposedly accidental overdose, and this man bought the house. I haven't talked with him that much, although I often see him walking along the perimeter of his land with his dog."

She'd been completely unaware. She'd thought he was a responsible pet owner. Obviously, his motivations were not quite so benign.

"I would question the accidental nature of your neighbor's death." She shuddered at Ryan's response. He reached out. The warmth of his hand on her face as he turned it toward him helped calm her, although it did little to dispel the chill that had settled in her soul. "Elise, honey, I think we both know that he's been watching you."

* * *

The man had been watching her for two months.

The rage that filled Ryan was unlike anything he'd ever experienced. Every time he considered that Elise, sweet with a dash of spice in her personality, had a contract on her life, his anger kindled anew. To learn that the man had been watching her, though, made it worse. The evil of it sickened him. He calmed himself, but it wasn't easy. Only the thought that he didn't want to offend Elise with the intensity of his feelings helped him regain control.

The squeal of brakes followed by a crash made him look up. A large van had spun, blocking the other side of the bridge. An unsuspecting car had rammed into its side.

Two men bounded down from the van. Both carried assault rifles. A third sauntered around the other side.

The three men started moving. Slowly they made their way down the bridge. One car started to back up. One of the men raised his rifle and shot out the tires. The people on the bridge started screaming. The one man forced the people in the first car to exit, holding his gun on them as they lined up inside the bridge.

"They're looking for me," Elise whispered. Her voice was thick with guilt. At least she wasn't panicking. He needed her clearheaded if they were going to get out of this.

"Yes, they are. But they are not going to find you."

Carefully he opened his door and slid out. He beckoned her to follow. They were far enough back and close enough to the side of the road that their actions were not immediately noticed.

"Ryan, we can't abandon these people." He grimaced at the reproach in her voice.

"We're not," he shot back. "My body camera is on, I sent an alert to the chief as soon as we noticed Hudson. The New Wilmington police should be here soon. But in the meantime, if those men recognize you, someone will get shot. And I don't think they much care if a civilian gets hurt, too."

"I could hide," Elise suggested, "and you could—"

"No," Ryan said firmly. "Even with my gun, there are too many of them for me to take out before they started firing back—and when that happened, there are too many innocent people who'd get caught in the cross fire. Me attacking them alone would just make things worse. It'll take a full squad of police officers to make them back down."

Leading her down the gravel-covered slope, he could hear her slipping and sliding behind him. He winced at a particularly loud slide. Twisting, he pulled her up close to the side of the hill and listened. The screaming and crying above was tugging at his conscience. He'd become a cop to protect people from danger like this, and it went against the grain to stand aside and do nothing. But he'd meant what he said. He was one man against five or more. If he'd stepped into the situation, it could have been explosive. People could have died.

The siren of the New Wilmington police broke the tension. He could hear the yells as the cops came from both directions. A gunshot was heard. Then he heard the rev of a motorcycle's engine, then a second one. There had been three motorcycles. Another gunshot, and the third motorcycle revved. A police siren leaving the scene told him clearly that one of the cruisers was giving chase.

A scraping sound alerted him that someone else was scurrying down the embankment. Pebbles scattered as the person slid down the slope. Adrenaline raced through Ryan's body. They'd come too far to be found now.

Grasping Elise's hand, he pulled her with him under the bridge. The cold water from the creek lapped up on the narrow bank, covering their feet. It was uncomfortable, but he was okay with that. He'd willingly suffer from wet, cold feet if it meant that Elise stayed alive.

A shout came from behind them. Ryan chanced a glance back to see that one of the men had indeed seen them and was giving chase. It was the same young man who had escaped back in LaMar Pond. The young man's face was twisted in a mixture of rage and evil glee. It was hard to believe someone that young could have so much hate inside them. It wasn't hard to draw the conclusion that he didn't intend for either of them to make it out of this alive.

Ironically, it was the rapt, fixated look on his face that gave Ryan hope. He'd found that when people gave in to their intense emotions, as the man rushing down the incline had so obviously done, they tended to lose their ability to reason and strategize. Which meant he might make a mistake.

The young man raised his gun, aiming it straight at Elise, clearly going for a fatal shot. *Not on my watch.* Ryan pushed her to the side. Elise fell, landing in the water, but the shot missed her. The man raised the gun, but Ryan fired before he had the opportunity to shoot again. The man fell. He didn't get up. It was impossible to tell if he was still breathing from where they stood.

Taking a life was never something Ryan took lightly. Not only because he was a police officer, trained to protect, but also because he'd grown up in a house of healers whose very calling was to save life.

They were in danger, but he still had to check on the man. Every nerve was taut. There was way too much happening just feet away. And he knew that at least three of the men were escaping on motorcycles. Sure, he hoped that the police would catch them. The practical side of him, however, was well aware that motorcycles had more maneuverability through narrow spaces than the police cruisers chasing after them. He doubted they'd catch all three.

Stepping carefully, he worked his way back to where the man lay and laid his fingers against the man's neck. He was still alive. But for how long? His pulse seemed thready. Ryan sent a quick text to the chief, describing their location and the man's condition. He knew the chief would make sure the New Wilmington police were alerted. There was nothing else to be done.

Which meant they had to keep moving. He rushed back to Elise, splashing water up his legs in his haste. Pulling Elise to her feet, he helped her to stand.

She was shivering, probably a mixture of cold and shock.

He needed to get her warm.

"Come on, honey. We need to keep moving. Who knows when those men will show up again. And we know that Hudson is in the area. We can't stay still."

A tear escaped and ran down her pale face. "I'm so cold, Ryan. And so tired. I still don't understand any of this. And I'm so worried for Mikey and Leah. Do you think they mean to kill them?"

How could he answer her? He ached to protect her, to comfort her. But she deserved the truth. He wouldn't disrespect her with lies. "I don't know. I hope that the fact that Hudson wants his son will protect Mikey at least."

He could tell that she understood what he'd left out. The only reason they were after Leah was because of Mikey. She wasn't important to the killers for anything else. Once they had Mikey, she'd be disposed of.

"Come on, honey. The quicker we move, the better chance we have of finding them first." He hated to push her, but he really needed to get her to a safe place. They kept close to the side of the bridge, hiding under it until the sirens from the police cars dwindled before fading completely. Even then, they walked quietly. Ryan was pretty sure that the killers wouldn't have gone far, especially if they suspected Elise was in the area.

As soon as he could, he got them into a wooded area. Unfortunately, there were still many open fields in the area. Ryan was sure he was going to hurt his neck, the way he had to keep looking around, constantly searching for dangers.

It wasn't just him, though. Elise was being vigilant, too.

"Do you think they're close?"

Again, he knew she deserved to know what he truly thought. "They haven't given up on you, if that's what you want to know. But neither have I. We'll keep going until we find your nephew."

He couldn't really promise that, but he did anyway. Because he knew that there wasn't any way that he'd stop looking. No matter the personal cost to him, he would do his best to get Elise and her nephew back together and out of danger—and get Leah Byler safely back to her family, too.

It was more than the fact that it was his job. Now his honor and even his emotions were too involved to do otherwise.

TEN

She'd be dead now if Ryan hadn't pushed her away.

Although she was frozen, colder than she could ever recall being in her life, Elise was grateful to be alive.

Thanks to the brave man striding at her side.

Another shudder coursed through her from the chill seeping into her bones. Her teeth were chattering so violently she could hear them. No matter how hard she rubbed her hands up and down her arms, she couldn't seem to get warm. It had been a hot day when they'd left LaMar Pond, but the temperature had dropped—and the sky had darkened alarmingly.

"We need to find a way to warm you up," Ryan said. She jumped guiltily. Surely, he had enough to worry about. "It's my fault. If I hadn't shoved you into the water—"

"If you hadn't shoved me, I would have been shot. Trust me, I'd much rather be cold and walking than dead."

He smiled slightly, but she could still read the concern in his eyes.

The jarring ring of his phone broke the tension.

"It's the chief again." He accepted the call. "Parker here."

His face darkened. *It can't be good news.* He stopped walking, his frown deepening. "Are you sure?…We're on foot. I had to abandon my truck beside the bridge…Will do."

He disconnected and turned to her. "I have good news and bad news. Want to hear the good news first?" She nodded. "The man I shot is still alive and has regained consciousness. Also, according to the chief, he's feeling talkative. He has no idea why you were targeted, but your house was bugged. And so was my cruiser. We were discussing where we were headed this morning before we changed vehicles."

Her jaw dropped. "How'd they know—"

"I was seen at your house the morning of the break-in. I wasn't aware of Dellon's connection to your case, or his location as your neighbor, but I do recall feeling as though I was being watched."

"I felt that way, too!" How could she have forgotten that?

"Yeah, well, he took pictures of me and my cruiser. It wasn't too hard to figure out who I was. So he tagged my vehicle. That's how he knew we were heading for the bridge. I mentioned my route when I was talking to the chief this morning. Anyway, he figured they'd cut us off at the pass, so to speak. They knew we were there. Fortunately, they didn't know what my off-duty vehicle was. Otherwise, they'd have headed straight toward us."

He took off his baseball cap and scratched the back of his head. "The bad news is that Dellon and two of his buddies got away. Dellon shot one of his own men to get the motorcycle. The police got the other one."

"And the people on the bridge?" She almost didn't want to know. She'd never forgive herself if anyone had been hurt, even though she hadn't been at fault.

"All fine. As soon as the police arrived, our brave criminals tried to run for it. There would have been no benefit in fighting the police, not when their target was nowhere in sight."

She winced.

"Hey, I didn't mean to sound so blasé about it." He moved close enough for his arm to brush hers.

Her eyes lifted to his face. How did one keep their distance when just standing this close made her forget how to breathe? "I know you didn't mean anything. It just hurts knowing I am the reason for people getting attacked, even if no one was hurt." Bending her head, she closed her eyes, blocking out the world for a moment. "When he attacked me, Hudson said that it was my fault my sister had died. I can't help wondering if he's right. I tried to get her to go to the police. What if she threatened Hudson with it?"

"Elise." This time, Ryan placed his warm hands on her shoulders. "You can't do that to yourself. Trust me, I know from experience. It will destroy you if you let yourself dwell on that."

She searched his face. He was holding something back. She could read the struggle clearly on his face. She waited. If he wanted to tell her, he would. It wasn't in her nature to force a confidence, but she could offer.

Like a friend would. They could be friends, right?

"If you want to tell me, I'll listen."

He hesitated, then took her hand and started walking again. She didn't break the silence because she could see his indecision. His head was down, and he continued frowning.

She had thought he'd decided against revealing anything further, but after five minutes of silence, he began to speak.

"I didn't grow up around here. I grew up in the southern part of the state. I would spend all day long with my best friend, Ricky. Man, from the time we met in third grade, we were inseparable. I was closer to Ricky than to my own brother. We would go everywhere together. Do anything we could to get a laugh. Or to get an adrenaline high. We were crazy stupid back then. Drove our folks batty with the stunts we'd pull. Never thought about what could happen, you know? We were invincible, nothing could hurt us."

A sad smile crossed his face as the memories took hold. She held her breath, silently willing him to continue. "Ricky and I even did some motorcycle races. I wiped out and broke my leg our junior year. My parents were not happy with me. Did I ever tell you that my father was doctor?"

"I don't remember if you told me that, but I do recall hearing that somewhere."

He nodded and sighed. "Yeah, he is from a long line of medical people. Mom, too. Even my brother became a doctor. I was supposed to be one, too. Only I had no interest in medicine. Zero. My dad, though, wouldn't even hear that. It never mattered what I said. I was going to be a doctor. And Ricky was just a bad influence.

"Don't get me wrong. My dad, he's a good guy. He chose medicine because he really wanted to help people. He's just stubborn. He was always after me to apply myself more." He deepened his voice and exaggerated his words, mimicking an older voice. "'You don't get into medical school with a D in geometry!'"

He shook his head. "I can hear him now. Always carrying on. As if med school was the only thing I could do. It wasn't *my* idea of where I belonged. Oh, no. I hated the idea. Hated the thought of patching up bones. And surgery? Made me nauseous just thinking about cutting people open."

She hesitated to break in. "What about your mother?"

"My mother is the sweetest woman on earth." She smiled. "It's true! Now, she never insisted on med school, but she always thought I should do something grand and important with my life. Instead of complaining about my grades, she would tell people about how well her son played the piano. 'Ryan could be a concert pianist,' she'd say. Gah! Didn't care for that idea, either. Let me tell you, I was not making my folks happy with my choices.

"I was always amazed that my dad allowed me to play the piano. I think she must have told him that it would give me steady hands."

She laughed quietly until his face darkened. "Anyway, when I was a senior, I was going through a rebellious stage, and my parents thought they needed to teach me a lesson, so they grounded me. Which meant I wasn't allowed to go the movies with my friends. I was so mad I snuck out of the house and walked over to Ricky's. He lived on our block. As I got closer, I heard a gunshot. I knew that the family didn't own a gun. I ran to the house just as a man wearing a ski mask ran out carrying a bag. I don't know what I was thinking. I shouted at him. He turned around and shot me in the leg, but it didn't slow me down. I tackled him—knocked him over. Other neighbors ran over to help. The police came. He was taken away."

This story wasn't going to end well, she knew. She could tell by the bleak tone of voice. She wasn't sure she wanted to know. But she had to keep listening. For him.

"I was taken to the hospital. My parents visited me. I expected to get yelled at for leaving the house. But they didn't yell at me. Instead, they informed me that my best friend was dead. He'd been shot when he'd interrupted the burglar robbing his family's house. And all I could think was that if I hadn't gotten grounded, we'd have been at the movies together, talking about girls and football."

The eyes he turned on her were haunted. "I know how it feels to blame yourself for someone's death. You can't, though. I had no idea what would happen. Neither did you. We can't see the future. And we aren't responsible for other people's choices."

Tears blinded her. The pain she'd seen in his face overwhelmed her. Needing to give him comfort, she moved close and put her arms around him. For a brief moment they comforted each other. Then he pulled back.

"Come on. Let's keep going. Maybe we'll find a house, someone who'll lend us a blanket or something."

She moved forward with him, but she couldn't just let it go. "Is that why you decided to become a cop?"

"Yes." He didn't look at her. "I wanted to make it up to Ricky at first. Then I realized that being a police officer is truly my calling. I believe it's what God wants me to do. Now I'm just trying to prove to my father that I'm not wasting my life."

She read his intensity. What also became clear was what he wasn't saying. Proving his worth—to his father, and maybe also to himself—was his sole focus right now. Which meant that he wasn't prepared to become involved with anyone. She should have been relieved.

Instead, she felt hollow.

He couldn't stand seeing her so miserable. If he had a coat to offer her, he would have. As it was, they had left everything in the truck. He couldn't regret that, as they would have surely died had they remained in the vehicle. Still, he winced as he heard her teeth chatter again.

They had kept away from the main roads as much as possible. It had been at least an hour since they'd seen another human being. He was anxious to find shelter now. It was going on evening. The temperature continued to drop. It was probably around sixty degrees now, but the biting wind made it feel much colder. Peering at the overcast sky, he judged that they were going to be stuck in a downpour in a few minutes. The low rumbles of thunder had moved closer and louder. And the wind had picked up.

The branches above them shook and swayed alarmingly. The farther they walked, the worse it got. Overhead, a couple of birds were attempting to fly. The wind resistance was so high they were practically flapping their wings in place.

Finally, he came upon a sight that gave him relief.

Up ahead was a small building. It was wooden and simply built. He knew what it was. They had come across an Amish schoolhouse. Whether or not it was still in use, he didn't know. What he did know was that it would provide them with shelter through the storm.

As they neared the school, the sounds of someone moving around inside could be heard.

Not wanting to startle anyone, Ryan knocked on the door. *Please, Lord, let them permit us to come in for shelter.*

The rustling sound inside stopped, but no one answered the door. Ryan knocked again. Footsteps could be heard moving toward the door. Just on the other side, they stopped. Ryan waited, but heard no answer. Perhaps they'd scared whoever it was?

"Hello?" he called, making his voice as kind as he could. "Sorry to bother you, but we were hoping to find a place to stay during the storm."

Silence. Feeling more than a little disappointed, he started to turn to his companion, ready to tell her they would have to keep looking. He hated to do that, looking into her pale face. She'd been a trouper, walking for the past two hours, but how much longer could she keep going?

The door opened, just a few inches, but enough for him to see the young woman inside. For a moment, he thought they'd found Leah. However, there was no sign of recognition from Elise. The woman pondered them for a moment, keeping the door firmly between them. Ryan didn't dare to move, lest she decide they couldn't be trusted.

Evidently, she saw nothing to alarm her, for she relaxed her hold on the door and swung it open.

"Hello," she said, her voice soft and pleasing. "I was preparing to return to my home."

"Please," Elise murmured, holding out a hand in supplication. The young Amish woman turned her attention to Elise. "We don't mean to disturb your plans. We are not from here. I fell in the creek earlier, and we've been walking for so long. We just want a place to stay while it storms."

The young woman, a girl really, nodded. She stepped back and motioned for them to enter. They did so quickly. Elise rubbed her hands up and down her arms. She opened her mouth to speak, but a sudden bout of shivering stopped her.

That seemed to decide their hostess. "Wait here. My *haus* is just behind. I will come back."

The girl walked out, closing the door behind her.

They were left alone again.

"Do you think she'll be back?" Elise's voice was almost monotone. She had to be exhausted.

"Even if she doesn't come back tonight, at least we have a dry place to stay."

Elise didn't respond. She moved to a desk and sat down. Crossing her arms on the smooth wooden surface, she lay her head down on them. Her lids dropped over her eyes, the long dark lashes contrasting against the pale skin.

He moved over and sat beside her, wrapping his arm around her shoulders. Maybe he could warm her up a bit.

He didn't know how much time passed before he heard a knock. Standing, he stepped quietly toward the door. It opened before he reached it and the young woman appeared again.

He moved to help her as she had her hands full. An armful of blankets was piled high in her arms. She stepped inside, and a young boy entered behind her. He was carrying a basket and a water jug. "It isn't much, but we brought some blankets to keep you warm and some food. I would let you stay at our home, but my *mam* is awful sick."

Ryan moved to take the blankets, smiling his thanks. "I understand. This is wonderful. We appreciate this very much. Honestly."

She ducked her head. "I'm Faith, and this is my brother, Jonas. We will be back tomorrow morning. I'm the teacher here. School starts at eight thirty."

He could see the question she didn't want to ask. "I'm sure we'll be on our way before then."

She started to leave with her brother.

"Wait!" Elise struggled to her feet.

"Jah?" Faith questioned.

"We have a pair of pictures to show you. My friend and my nephew. They've disappeared and they're in trouble. By any chance, have you seen them?"

Ryan obliged and pulled up the pictures of Leah and Mikey on his phone. He showed them to their hostess and her brother. He was disappointed yet unsurprised to find that neither of them showed any sign of recognizing either Leah or Mikey.

"It was a long shot," Ryan mused as he pushed his phone back into his pocket. "I was hoping since we know that Leah is from New Wilmington."

"I am sorry. I know the people in my community, but there are nineteen districts in New Wilmington."

Ryan nodded, trying not to be discouraged. He'd known it wasn't likely that the first people they met would recognize the two they were seeking. But nineteen districts? That was quite a lot of territory to cover. And there was no way they could ask to borrow a car. Or a bike. He didn't know much about the Amish, but he did know that some districts didn't allow bicycles. Or anything with rubber wheels.

"I am sorry I cannot help you find your friends. But I am glad I can offer you shelter—and food." Faith placed a basket on one of the desks. The smell of hot apples filled the air. After thanking their hosts, Ryan watched as they left before walking to Elise and placing a blanket around her shoulders. Her eyes were huge as they met his. He hated the hopelessness he could see in them.

"Don't give up. We are close now. The fact that we've seen Langor here proves that we are on the right track."

A sniff answered him. It was a poignant sound; he knew she was fighting tears, struggling with her sense of loss. Even in the darkening room, he could see the way her shoulders squared under the rough blanket, the set of her jaw as she lifted her chin.

"I know. I'm trying to trust God. It's taking all the faith I have, but I know that God is in control."

He lifted a hand to brush away a stray curl from her forehead. As he did so, the sweet, floral scent of her shampoo tantalized him. Distracting himself, he mused on her words. He couldn't remember not having faith, but guilt struck as he realized that he had sort of taken God's help for granted lately.

"My mother loves to quote that verse—you know that one that says, 'If God be for us, who can be against us?'" He made quotes in the air with his fingers.

"Romans 8:31. I was actually repeating that verse to myself earlier today as we walked."

Admiration for the beautiful woman seated in front of him grew. Had he ever met a more remarkable person? Her strength, her determination to keep going, amazed and inspired him.

He was losing his fight against his heart, and at the moment, he couldn't bring himself to care. But he *needed* to care. For her sake as much as his. He had nothing to offer her when he knew he had so much to accomplish before he could allow himself to find a bride.

A bride? Had he really just thought that? Yes, he had. In his mind, he could imagine himself introducing Elise and Mikey to his family. He could see the amazing mother she would be. Already was, in fact.

The depths of her smoky hazel eyes beckoned him.

He was drawn in. He held back for a few seconds, but then he caved, leaning in and touching her lips with his. She went still for a minute. Stiffened in shock. Then she relaxed and leaned into the kiss. It was a movement of acceptance that filled him with joy.

He acknowledged to himself that he'd been wanting to do this since the moment they'd met.

ELEVEN

The last thing Elise had expected was for Ryan to kiss her. But when he'd looked at her with such warmth and affection in his chocolate-brown eyes, all her resistance had melted. The first touch of his lips was soft. She could taste the cinnamon gum he'd been chewing earlier. He moved away slightly, searching her face to gauge her reaction before bringing his mouth back to hers for a second, deeper kiss. She was shivering again, but not from the cold. It was a chaste kiss, but she knew she'd remember it forever. Treasure it, because that's all she could ever have from him.

When he pulled back, she could sense that their relationship had changed. She could also see that he was thinking about all the reasons he shouldn't have kissed her. She couldn't blame him. She was doing the same thing.

She'd sensed the strength of his love for his family. He might be going through a strained period with his parents, but the love and respect was vibrant in his voice when he spoke of them. In time, those wounds would heal. He would realize that he didn't need to prove himself—to them or anyone else. And then, Ryan would feel free to invest himself in a relationship. A relationship that would naturally lead to marriage and kids. A relationship that couldn't be with her. If she'd learned anything from her ex-fiancée, it was how unsuited she was for that role.

The pain of it nearly bowled her over. She had to hold on to the fact that she knew God had a plan. If only it included Ryan.

Enough! She was not one who gave in to self-pity.

To distract them both, she nodded her head toward the basket. "What's in there?"

Relief crossed his face as he rose to bring the basket closer. Inside, there were thick slices of bread, a crock of butter, hot sliced apples, some sort of chicken and noodle soup and a jug of water, along with plates, bowls, utensils and soft cloth napkins. Elise helped herself to everything except the chicken and noodles, almost crying in relief as the hearty food settled in her cold, empty stomach. She couldn't remember ever being as famished as she'd been today.

After they ate, they pulled out the blankets. The sooner they could get to sleep, the better. Knowing that schoolchildren would be arriving early in the morning, they needed to be up and on their way before they arrived.

Ryan settled down a few feet away from her. The night was dark. The clouds hid the moonlight. Still, she was aware of him lying a mere few feet from her. As she closed her eyes, she said a brief prayer, thanking God for protecting them both that day, and asking Him to hold Mikey and Leah in His hands.

The hard floor made for a very uncomfortable bed. She couldn't find a position she liked. It didn't matter. Elise was so exhausted she drifted off to sleep, regardless.

* * *

The building shook.

Elise shot upright, her heart pounding, as the room around her swayed and creaked. A bright slash lit the sky outside. Thunder crashed, shaking the room again. The rain pounded on the roof.

She could smell the fresh rain. It was a smell she'd always loved. She didn't love it now, though. The small schoolhouse, which had seemed so secure and sheltering a few hours earlier, now seemed frail as the violence of the storm outside grew. Minute by minute, she sat in the darkness, arms looped around her knees, listening as the storm raged. The thunder would move off, only to return as a new system rolled through. Several times, she heard the crashes of falling tree limbs outside the walls of the schoolhouse. She'd lived in Pennsylvania long enough to know that nature was wreaking havoc on the landscape.

How could Ryan sleep through this? A snort echoed in the room. Elise snickered. Yet sleeping he was. Every now and then, a soft snore would emerge from where he had fallen asleep, just a few feet beyond her. Annoyance that he could sleep during the chaos while she was wide-awake dissolved into amusement. In a weird way, she was grateful for the little noises he made while he slept. The room around them was so dark, if she didn't have that intermittent proof that he was there, she might have wondered if he'd left while she was sleeping.

Thud.

What was that? Probably nothing to worry about, and yet the amusement she'd been holding in vanished. The wind level had again increased. It whistled and moaned as the windows rattled. Inanely, she thought that she'd never realized that the Amish had glass windows.

Suddenly, she hated being alone with her own thoughts.

"Ryan," she whispered as loudly as she could, then laughed at herself. If the storm outside wouldn't wake him, a whisper from her wouldn't, either. Since she was intent on waking him up, she should just go ahead and talk. She took a deep breath and said his name again, louder this time.

"Ryan!"

Another flash of lightning lit up the room. For an instant, she was able to see as Ryan bolted to a sitting position.

"What!"

She crawled over to where he was. Suddenly, though, she felt shy. And absurd. She was a grown woman. Why was she allowing an insignificant storm to mess with her mind? As the building shook again, she amended her thoughts. This was no small storm. Another loud crack split the night. She recognized the sound of a tree being blown over seconds before they heard the distinctive sound of the trunk slamming against the schoolhouse.

Elise shrieked as part of the roof was pushed inward, along with broken branches. Glass shattered as the pressure caused the windows to cave in. Instantly, the rain pelted inside, and the chill invaded the building. Ryan took charge, pulling them both over to the other side of the building. Using his phone for light, he shoved a table up against the brick chimney and motioned for Elise to slide under it, to be at least partially sheltered from the cold and the rain. He took a large blanket and covered the table with it. Elise was reminded of the tents she and Mikey would make in the living room. A few minutes later, he was under the table with her. Sitting with his back against the bricks, he pulled her to his side and covered them with several of the blankets.

Elise nestled inside the warmth of the cocoon he'd built for them. While she knew it was only a couple of blankets, the little tent he'd made for them provided the illusion of safe haven from the storm. Comforted and pleasantly enveloped in warmth, she leaned her head on his chest, closing her eyes again as the steady beat of his heart soothed her like a lullaby. Exhausted, she allowed her lids to drift. Within minutes, she was sleeping.

What was he supposed to do now?

A cramp gripped his leg, but he was unable to stretch it out. Not without waking Elise. She'd been through so much in the past few days he knew that she hadn't been sleeping well. The purple smudges under her lovely eyes had become darker and more vivid with each day. And if he wasn't mistaken, she'd also lost a few pounds.

He shook his head. Of course she'd lost weight. Her nephew, who she loved like her own child, was missing; the man she believed murdered her sister was after her and had tried to kill her; and now she'd found out that some gang had decided she'd be better off dead, as well. Who would be able to eat and sleep normally?

The cramp expanded, pain radiating down his left

leg, the one that had been shot so many years ago. He should have known better than to sit on a hard floor with his knees bent. This always happened. Gritting his teeth, he softly tapped the back of his head against the bricks, trying to keep the groan that had settled in his throat from escaping.

Maybe if he could shift a little, he'd be able to stretch the limb without disturbing Elise. Slowly he leaned to the right, taking his weight on his right hip and leg as much as possible. Elise shifted with him and stirred. He stilled and held his breath. She sighed and then was quiet. Gently letting out the breath he'd been holding, Ryan slowly extended his leg. The pain pulsed. He stopped for a moment, allowing the fierce ache to ease to a dull throb. Then he continued until the leg was completely extended.

With the pain no longer dominating his thoughts, he started wondered what time it was it. He reached for his phone with his other hand. For a moment, the little cave he'd made was brightly lit. It was almost dawn. Soon the sun would begin to rise. The rain had softened to a low patter, but the wind continued to howl.

In a few hours, the children would arrive to find that their school had a tree on top of it.

Hopefully, he and Elise would be on their way before that happened. They needed to keep searching for Leah and Mikey. Who knew how many of the other eighteen districts they'd go through before meeting up with someone who knew her?

He wasn't looking forward to the day ahead. He would, however, do whatever he had to do to erase the sadness from the face of the woman sleeping on his chest. The woman he was dangerously close to falling for.

No. He couldn't fall for Elise. Sure, she was beautiful and brave, smart and funny. Not to mention a woman of faith, which was paramount to him. If he was ready to settle down, she'd be perfect for him. But at present, he had nothing to offer her. Nothing to offer Mikey. At twenty-seven, he was still new enough on the police force that his work hours were less than ideal. He lived in an apartment. And he still hadn't earned his father's approval.

If you'd become a doctor, like he'd wanted, none of this would be an issue.

He shoved that thought aside, refusing to give it credence. He knew he'd needed to become a cop. Ricky deserved it.

He stilled. Was he a cop because of a debt he thought he owed rather than because God wanted him to be? He'd told Elise yesterday that she couldn't blame herself for her sister's murder, had even told her his story, but had he been honest with himself?

Was being a cop his idea, or God's?

He wrestled with the thought, his thoughts going around and around in circles. Doubt crept into his mind. He'd been so stubborn, so sure of himself. What if he was wrong?

He was so mired in his thoughts that at first he didn't recognize the sound for what it what.

Then understanding struck.

"Elise! Wake up! Now!"

Elise woke up immediately at his shout, the top of her head banging into his nose. Spots danced in front of his eyes as pain ricocheted through his head.

"Sorry!" she cried.

"I'm fine. Listen to that, Elise. We're in trouble."

Reaching out, he pulled back the blanket covering the table enough for the barest hint of dawn light to seep through. He saw her expression, first confused, then awash with horror as she realized what was happening. A sound like the roar of a freight train surrounded them.

There were no train tracks anywhere near them.

They were sitting ducks in the middle of a field, in a tiny Amish schoolhouse, while a tornado touched down.

They were out of time. Ryan grabbed hold of the blanket and pulled it back over the opening. It would keep flying glass off them at the very least. Then he pulled Elise close to the ground, covering her as much as he could.

He could hear her whispering a prayer. He added his own "Amen" to it.

In his worst nightmares, he'd never imagined the sounds around him as the tornado ripped the world apart. The building shuddered as something landed against its side, hard. Probably another tree. The roar of the twister would seem to fade, then it would come back. He could feel Elise trembling as he held her.

Then it happened. The roar of the twister was directly overhead. He prayed it would leave without touching the schoolhouse. For a moment, he thought it would when the sound moved to the right. But then…

Slam!

For as long as he lived, Ryan would never forget the ripping noise as the tornado smashed into the small schoolhouse and the walls collapsed inward. The table above them cracked as the weight of the destroyed structure collapsed in on it. The air grew heavy.

Then silence reigned again.

The tornado was gone as fast as it had struck. Elise's breathing was the only sound. He frowned as he listened. Her breathing wasn't just loud. It was harsh. Almost rusty sounding.

"Elise? Honey, the tornado's gone. Are you all right?"

She coughed, then choked.

She was desperately allergic to dust. He remembered her telling him that several days ago. That was why she'd hired Leah to clean her house and probably why she had wood floors instead of carpeting. Right now, she sounded almost asthmatic. He'd heard the sound of an asthma attack before. Jace's wife, Melanie, had asthma, and he'd been present for one of her attacks. The way Elise was breathing, well, it sure sounded a lot like Melanie's.

A new fear gripped him. He shoved himself free, hoping that the debris left by the tornado was loose enough that he could shift it and work his way out to free them. He was able to lift the blanket slightly. Using the flashlight app on his phone, he could see a wall of wooden debris had fallen on them. Could he make a hole through which they could crawl out?

He pushed and shoved at the blanket. Nothing. It wouldn't budge. And Elise's breathing sounded worse.

Had they come all this way to die? He refused to give in. Straining as much as he could, he continued to shove, all the while listening to Elise.

"Honey? Elise?"

"Ryan, it hurts," she gasped, her voice faint.

"You stay with me, hear? I'm gonna get us out. You hold on."

Nothing.

"Elise? Elise!"

She didn't respond. With his heart in his throat, he kept digging, praying that someone would come for them before Elise died, buried alive.

TWELVE

Ryan was ready to cry in relief when he heard people yelling around the schoolhouse. The debris shifted and creaked as it was lifted, board by board. It felt like forever, but he could hear the voices getting closer.

"Mr. Ryan?"

Faith had come back. "Faith! We're buried near the chimney. Elise is hurt."

Feet stomped closer. Another few minutes passed before the table was finally pushed aside. Ryan lifted Elise off the floor and passed her to the hands that reached for her.

He hovered over her as she stirred. The fresh air, cool but not cold, seemed to help. She was breathing, and the rasp had lessened. No thanks to him. For all his promises, he really hadn't kept her safe, had he? After a few minutes, her long lashes fluttered open and he saw the dazed expression on her face fade as comprehension took its place.

He could see her shock as she gazed over his shoulder.

He turned. And whistled silently. He'd been so concerned about her, he'd not taken the time to assess the destruction. And it was vast. The schoolhouse was demolished.

"I guess they won't have school today," a weak voice joked.

He slanted a grin at Elise. His girl was quick to return to her own sassy self.

Only she wasn't his girl. He really needed to remember that.

"We won't have school today, it is so."

Elise and Ryan both swung their heads to face the speaker. Elise's face grew pink. Ryan could sympathize. She wouldn't have made the comment if she'd known that Faith was close by.

"I didn't mean to be callous," Elise apologized, coughing slightly. "I just, I don't know. Sometimes it's easier for me to deal with shock with a joke. It probably wasn't appropriate."

Faith offered her a small smile. "Please. It is fine. I told my family about you last night. When we heard the tornado, my *dat*—" she indicated a bearded man walking along the edge of the demolished school "—he notified my brothers and my *oncle*."

Ryan's throat tightened as he looked around. At least fifteen people had gathered around to help. Mostly men and boys, but there were three girls, aside from Faith, who had gathered.

"Your family saved our lives," Ryan said. "I was trying, but I know there was no way I could have dug us out. We would have been buried alive."

Faith ducked her head, a shy smile on her face. "It is what needed to be done, *jah*? I think Gott had a reason why I needed to return to the schoolhouse last night. It was Gott who saved you. He is a *gut* provider."

Ryan nodded his head. He couldn't argue with that line of thinking. God had come through for them yet again.

Faith's father approached. "I understand from my *tochtor*, Faith, that you are searching for a woman and a child."

"Yes, sir."

Elise bumped gently into Ryan's side as she came to stand beside him. He inhaled her floral scent, now mingled with dust, and thought he'd never smelled anything better. "My nephew is the child," she explained. "We believe that Leah is trying to keep him safe. They are both in danger."

The man frowned, concern growing on his face as he looked at his own daughter.

Ryan hurried to reassure him. "We will be leaving soon. It is not our intent to bring trouble your way."

"That is *gut*. Maybe so we can provide you with some food before you leave."

"Excuse me, Dat. May I speak?" The small group switched their attention to Faith.

Surprised, the older man cast her a questioning glance. "*Jah*, what would you say?"

The young woman shifted, and Ryan got the distinct impression that she wasn't used to having the attention of so many adults focused on her at once. His initial impression of a shy young woman was confirmed by her rosy cheeks.

"I wonder me, if I use the buggy, I could drive them around a bit today. I won't be teaching today.

I would enjoy helping them. It would be better if I drove them."

When the father didn't look convinced, she continued. "I could take my brother, too. Dat, the nephew is *kind*."

There weren't many German words that he knew, but he was pretty sure that *kind* meant child. He became aware of Elise squeezing his arm. It was probably painful for her not to add in her own arguments. Her face sparkled with new hope. If he had to guess, he would say she approved of the idea of having a way to get around to the other local districts. They wouldn't be able to visit all eighteen, but maybe they wouldn't need to if they hit on the right district today. And even if they didn't, they'd cover more territory and eliminate some options.

Faith's father reached a decision. "*Jah*, you may go, but not alone. Your *bruder* Isaac will go with you. Be back by the evening meal."

"*Jah*, Dat. I will." Faith beckoned to Elise and Ryan. They began to follow her. "Come. We will eat at my *oncle*'s *haus* before we leave."

Breakfast was a simple meal. Homemade muffins and fruit, with some milk to wash it down. There was little talk beyond Faith telling them that the tornado had caused more damage to homes and several of the local Amish businesses. The community would be busy that day cleaning up the mess.

"When you eat all, come to the buggy. I will get the horses ready." Isaac stood. He was a tall youth of about eighteen. His clean-shaven face was proof that he was unmarried. He nodded respectfully to his family before hurrying outside to prepare for the journey.

Under the table, Ryan reached out and touched Elise's hand. Surprised, she swiveled her head to meet his eyes, a question in hers.

"Are you well?" He kept his voice down, not wanting to disrupt the others.

She nodded. "Yes. I'm anxious to get moving, and my chest hurts a little from coughing, but other than that I'm well."

He frowned, blaming himself for her discomfort. When the others got up, he started to follow. Elise's hand on his arm stopped him.

"What's wrong?"

He sighed. "Elise, you could have died in there. And I couldn't help you. If I'd been the doctor my father wanted me to be, maybe I could have saved you some suffering. Instead, I had to listen to you struggling just to breathe, knowing I was useless to you!"

Those lovely eyes widened. She reached out and put a hand on his cheek. "That's the dumbest thing I've ever heard." He tried to move away. She wouldn't let him. She had a strong grip for someone so slender. "I'm serious. Have you stopped to consider that if not for you I wouldn't have been alive before the tornado? Ryan, your being a cop has already saved me. I think you need to take your own advice and remember that God's got this."

Shame seeped into his pores. *Sorry, God.* Immediately, peace swept away the guilt. He leaned forward to kiss her forehead. "Thanks, Elise. I guess I needed to hear that."

It was another twenty minutes before they were on their way. "You should ride in the back." Isaac held open the door for them.

That made sense, so they climbed in. Isaac and his sister sat on the bench seat in front. Their voices were too soft to hear as they traveled. As for Ryan, it was amazing how intimate the inside of the buggy felt. He tried without much success to keep his mind from reliving the kiss they'd shared the night before in the schoolhouse. It seemed much longer than fifteen hours since they'd shared that special moment.

The morning was full of disappointment. They drove to so many homes and businesses that they started to blend together.

When they crossed over the Banks Covered Bridge again, Ryan noticed that Elise tensed. "Do you think they're far away?" she whispered.

No need to guess who *they* was.

"I would be surprised if they were still here, knowing the police are on the lookout for them."

Five hours later, they stopped at yet another business, an Amish store. The small group went inside, pausing to let their eyes adjust to the darker interior. The store was small, but the shelves were packed. Baking goods, canned goods, candy... Ryan was impressed with the sheer variety kept on hand.

He followed Elise to the front counter. A woman stood watch, smiling at them while keeping a careful eye on the small child, probably around a year old, napping in a portable crib. He couldn't help it. He flashed a small smile at the child. Someday, he'd be a father if God had it in His plan. Ryan cast a glance at Elise. Realizing he was treading on dangerous ground, he forced himself to look away from her.

Elise's hand trembled as she used her phone to show the kind-faced young woman the pictures of

Leah and Mikey. The woman gasped, her hands flying to her mouth. Tears filled her blue eyes.

"Leah! *Jah*, I know her! That's my friend, Leah!"

Elise sagged against the counter.

Finally! She had begun to think they'd never meet anyone who'd recognize Leah. Now, to find someone who not only recognized her but knew her well, Elise's bruised heart soaked up the hope. Her sagging spirits lifted.

"Ma'am, have you seen her in the past few days?" Ryan stepped up to the counter, his hand resting on Elise's back.

She was grateful for the comforting touch. She'd felt so lost for so long. His presence had helped her hold on to her courage in the face of the adversity they'd come up against.

The young woman smiled at her, the smile tinged with sadness. "*Nee*, she left soon after her parents died. She went to stay with a cousin."

Elise nodded. "Yes, I know. We talked with him."

"Maybe you should try her brother's *haus*?" the woman suggested. "He is close by."

Immediately brightening, Elise nodded eagerly. "That sounds like a fantastic idea. Would you have the address?"

If she could get the address, she could plug it into her phone. She looked at her phone. Oh. Maybe not. Her battery was low. The map feature would drain it in minutes. She glanced at Ryan. He seemed to know what was on her mind as he held up his own phone and shook his head, grimacing. Then he half smiled, apologetic. "Sorry, sweetheart. No can do. My phone is completely dead."

"I do not know the address," the woman murmured, her smile tinged with regret. "I will write directions for you, would that be *gut*?"

Appreciating the help, Elise nodded. The woman got down a pad of paper and began to draw a map. The baby in the crib woke and soon she was sobbing, her little chin wobbling as tears ran down her face.

"May I hold her for a minute?" Elise asked, hoping she wasn't committing some huge faux pas.

Apparently not, for the young mother bent and picked up the child before handing her over to Elise. Diverted, the baby stopped crying and stared at Elise with enormous brown eyes. She popped a chubby thumb into her mouth, her gaze never wavering from Elise.

After finishing her drawing, the young mother pushed the map toward them. Elise glanced at it, then handed her precious cargo back to the woman.

"Denke," she murmured, accepting her child. The little girl twisted to keep Elise in her sights. "I hope you find Leah. She is a *gut* friend."

"Thank you. I hope we do, too." Anxiety colored her voice, but she couldn't help it. She liked being in control, but it had been so long since she'd felt she had any control over the circumstances in her life.

Turn it over to God. She took a deep breath, thanked the woman again, then left. Isaac and Faith had already returned to the buggy. Elise appreciated the way they gave them privacy.

"You looked good in there," Ryan said.

Huh? She raised an eyebrow at him.

"With the baby. You're a natural."

Pain caught her unawares. She stiffened her back and tried to smile, but she could feel her lips tremble. Without responding, she thrust the map into Ryan's hands before hurrying to the brown covered buggy. Climbing inside, she strove to calm herself before Ryan joined her. She could hear him giving the map to the Amish siblings and explaining what the woman in the store had told them.

The pain and sadness from her experiences with Brady that had been shoved to the back of her mind for so long bubbled to the top and wouldn't be forced back. For too long, she'd denied or ignored the agony that had once ripped her whole world apart. She couldn't ignore it anymore. Having Ryan unknowingly rub it in her face so out of the blue, well, it was the last straw for her.

The door opened, and he climbed up beside her. The buggy jerked forward. Her shoulder bumped into his. Still struggling, she kept her face turned toward the window. For a full five minutes, they were silent.

"Okay..." Ryan drew the word out, breaking the thick silence that lay between them. "This is awkward. I have no clue what happened back there. I obviously offended you, but I don't know how, so all I can say is that I'm so sorry I upset you."

She shrugged, holding up a hand. He quieted. She knew he was still watching her. It didn't take much imagination to picture the crease that was probably wrinkling his brow.

He didn't deserve the silent treatment from her. She knew that she was being unfair. For the first time, she realized she wanted to share her sorrow, to tell someone else the story.

She decided just to tell it straight. Maybe it was like when you tore off a bandage fast. If she just told it quickly maybe it wouldn't hurt so much.

"Elise?" It bothered her that she was responsible for the doubt, for the uncertain tone in his deep voice.

"I'm okay." She twisted in her seat, facing the man that she was growing to care for too much for the well-being of her heart. She drew in a deep breath, letting the oxygen filling her lungs steady her nerves. There. She dove in. "I was engaged to be married once. Four years ago. Before Karalynne died. I thought I had met the perfect guy. I was in college. He was older. Working his way toward partnership in a law firm. I thought we were the perfect couple. Everyone said so." She bit her lip, remembering how she'd been so blind.

"But when we were alone, he was always...he called it 'correcting' me...because in his eyes, I was always doing something wrong. He had an image to maintain, you know? And I needed to make sure that I enhanced that image. I kept telling myself that it would get better. I'd learn what he expected and then I'd know better than to always mess things up."

A humorless laugh escaped.

"I was so dumb. In my defense, I was young, and my sister and I had been bounced around so much, I just wanted some security. Someone to love me."

His hand gripped hers. "Elise, you don't have to tell me if you don't want to."

How could she have imagined that Brady was compassionate? Listening to the velvet warmth of Ryan's voice, gazing into his face, open with sympathy, she knew that Brady had never been anything but selfish.

"No, I want to. I've never told anyone, but I think I want you to know. To understand." Using her free hand, she pushed back her hair from her face. "We were three weeks out from the wedding, and I wasn't feeling well. Nothing I could define. Just a general feeling of blah." She made a face. "I wanted to go to the doctor. He insisted I was fine, that it was just wedding nerves." She shook her head. "I can hardly believe that I allowed someone to control me to that extent. But I did. He didn't want me to go to the doctor, so I didn't. Two days later, my appendix ruptured. It was bad. Then infection set in, and it took me a long time to recover. When he told me the wedding was off, at first I thought he was being considerate. Postponing it until I was better."

She paused. Her stomach turned. She'd come to the worst part.

"Let me guess. Prince Charming wasn't postponing. What, did he blame you for messing up his schedule by getting sick?"

She smiled slightly at his sarcastic words. "Something like that. I hadn't lived up to his idea of what a wife should be. He said that he realized I would be a hindrance in his efforts to make partner. I was, he claimed, unfit to be a wife."

"That's baloney!" Ryan burst out. "What an idiot. Elise, he's the one who was unfit, not you. You're beautiful, smart, caring. He was a clod. You're better off without him."

Warmth coursed through her at his defense, but she wasn't done.

She needed to tell him the last part. How the burst appendix and the infection had damaged her.

A sudden yell jerked both their heads up. Isaac yanked the buggy to a halt.

And that's when Elise saw that her nightmares were coming true. Hudson Langor had found them. He had forced the buggy to a stop and was walking toward them with a gun. Ryan started to reach back for his own gun. He stopped when Hudson yanked Faith down from the buggy seat.

They all froze as he held the gun to her side.

THIRTEEN

He couldn't believe this was happening. He'd been so involved in Elise's story he hadn't noticed the car Hudson was driving pulling in front of them, blocking them to force them into stopping.

Well, he was in a pickle now. That was for sure. If he drew his gun, or made any sudden moves, Faith would be shot, possibly killed. He slid his eyes to the side, attempting to gauge Isaac's reaction. Although the youth was pale, he didn't display any other signs of fear.

Okay, Lord, how am I supposed to get out of this? Please help me save these people.

Ryan knew there was a high probability that he would not survive this encounter. Given Hudson Langor's history, it was doubtful he'd have any compunction about shooting anyone who got in his way, which Ryan intended to do. Did the man know that he was a cop? It was still unclear whether he and Dellon were acting together or not.

"Elise!" Hudson Langor shouted. "I know you're in there, girl! I followed you from that little store. Get out here, or this girl will die. You know I'll do it!"

"Let me out, Ryan." Elise slid closer to him. "I can't let him shoot her."

Man, he wanted to tell her no. But he couldn't think of another option.

"I'll let you out. But I am going to be looking for an opportunity to take him down. Do your best not to get directly in front of him."

She nodded.

"Elise!" Hudson's voice was growing wild. No telling what he'd do.

"I'm coming, Hudson. Don't shoot her."

"Wait, you don't have a gun on you, do you?" Suspicion was thick in Hudson's dark, angry voice.

"You know I don't like guns."

She was stalling for time. Ryan knew it. He could only pray that Hudson wouldn't decide to take offense and shoot.

Ryan angled himself to get a better view of the situation. This was his first chance to get a truly thorough look at Hudson Langor. The man didn't resemble his driver's license picture in the least. And it wasn't just the facial scarring, although that was significant. No, the man from the photos had appeared charming, confident.

The man holding the gun on Faith was sweating profusely. He seemed almost maniacal. His hair, what hadn't been destroyed, was standing on end. The hand holding the gun didn't look steady. If Ryan had the opportunity to catch Hudson unawares, he would act. But he'd have to be careful. The last thing he wanted to do was put Isaac or Faith in any more harm.

Or Elise.

His heart thudded hard, filling his ears with its pounding, at the thought of Elise being harmed.

Elise stepped out of the buggy and onto the pavement. Ryan's breath stuttered to a halt. He thought his chest would explode with the force of his emotions. *Put them aside, Parker. She needs you to be calm and clearheaded.* Unfortunately, memories of Ricky surfaced, setting his teeth on edge.

He couldn't fail Elise. Not now.

Sucking in a calming breath, he forced himself to relax.

"You there!" Hudson yelled, spittle shooting from his mouth with the force of his shout. He waved the gun in Ryan's direction. *Great.* Madman swinging a gun. Ryan cringed, praying the gun wouldn't go off in the man's agitated state. "Out here where I can keep an eye on you! And leave your hands where I can see them."

Taking care not to make any movements that would startle the man, Ryan climbed from the buggy, his eyes never leaving Hudson's face. It was difficult. The itch to check on Elise, to make sure she was okay, was strong, but Ryan controlled it.

Right now, his reactions were the only things he could control, a fact that he didn't like one little bit.

Once his feet were firmly on the ground, Hudson glared at him. "You have the look of a cop. I don't like cops. I bet you have a gun on you, don't you?"

Hudson yanked Faith closer. "Take it out, drop it on the ground and kick it away."

Ryan didn't even make the token protest. His gun was partially visible, anyway. Hating to give up his weapon, Ryan still did as the man said. He had to if he had any hope of keeping Hudson from shooting anyone.

"Okay, here it is." Giving the service revolver a nudge with his foot, Ryan sent it a few feet to the side. Hopefully, he'd have a chance to make a dive for it. He promised himself he wouldn't hesitate if an opportunity to disarm the man appeared.

Faith made a tiny gasp as Hudson dug the gun back into her side. Other than that, the Amish girl stayed still.

"Hudson, let her go. You know she doesn't have anything to do with this." Elise's soft voice trembled as she pleaded with her brother-in-law. Although he applauded her effort, Ryan felt the likelihood of Hudson releasing the girl was slim. Not when she could be used to force the others to comply.

He was right. Hudson just sneered at his late wife's sister. The hate on his face was enough to make one shudder.

"You must be stupid, Elise." Hudson's tone was scathing. "But then, you never were too bright. It's no wonder that lawyer fellow dropped you. Why would I release her? She's my insurance that you'll give me what I want."

From the corner of his eye, Ryan could see Elise clench her fists. "I don't have what you want."

"I know you have that SD card. I need it! And I want my son!" he nearly howled. "Thanks to you, I have no wife, and my former boss is hunting me down. But I still have my son. Where is he?"

The final words came out in a roar.

This was it. The man had finally lost all control.

"What do you mean, your boss is hunting you?" Elise demanded. "Is that the man who is watching me?"

For a moment, Hudson looked startled. "I have no clue who's watching you. All I know is that you took the evidence that could prevent me from starting over—and you took my boy. I want them back. That SD card has what I need to bargain with my boss. Now, where are they? Tell me right now, or this pretty girl here dies!"

"Langor, don't make this worse for yourself than it already is!" Ryan called out.

Hudson ignored him.

"I don't have Mikey right now, Hudson. Surely you can see that," Elise replied. "And I never had the SD card. Karalynne never gave it me. If she had I would have turned it in to the police long ago."

Hudson lifted the gun until it was level with Faith's head. The group gasped collectively. At the last moment, Hudson backed up, moving his hand higher on her arm to grasp it better.

Everything happened at once. As his grasp loosened, Faith shrieked and jerked her arm away. Hudson shot the gun. The bullet went wild, slamming into the side of the buggy. The horse startled, rearing, jarring the buggy and throwing Isaac to the ground. Ryan saw Elise grab a handful of gravel from the road and toss it straight in Langor's face. As the man screamed and scratched at his face and eyes, Ryan took a long running leap, knocking the man off his feet. His gun skittered several feet away.

It took some wrestling, but Ryan managed to subdue Hudson Langor. Unfortunately, he didn't have any handcuffs on him. They'd gotten lost in the mess back at the schoolhouse.

"Isaac, do you carry any rope, or anything we could use to bind his hands?" Ryan was a bit out of breath from his skirmish with the heavier man.

"Jah." The Amish youth seemed remarkably unfazed by all that had happened. He had been soothing the horse—which, thankfully, hadn't bolted—but at Ryan's words, he reached into a box under the seat of the buggy. He brought out a long rope. A clothesline, Ryan thought.

Within minutes, Langor was tied up.

"Now what?" Elise questioned.

Ryan was humbled by the trust he saw reflected in her gaze. After all that had happened, this amazing woman still trusted him. It was an honor he wouldn't take for granted.

"Now we have to find a way to let the police know to come and get him."

"Maybe put him in the buggy?" Isaac tilted his head. "We can drive him to town."

Ryan shook his head. "I appreciate the offer, Isaac. But I don't want to have any of you closed in the buggy with him." He thought for a moment. "If you could go into town with your sister, and have the police called, that would be a huge help. Then you and your sister can head for home. Elise and I will wait with him."

The young siblings agreed. They'd dealt with more danger than they'd expected this day. Ryan was grateful. More than grateful. He admired their courage and their common sense, but they were still teenagers. And their father was waiting for them at home.

They found an out-of-the-way area where Elise and Ryan could sit in the shade and wait for the police.

Settling Hudson down against a tree, Ryan wrapped more rope around the tree, further ensuring that Hudson was trapped. He and Elise then stepped back up to the road to say their goodbyes to Faith and Isaac. Isaac took the time to revise the map they had, showing a smoother path, as it was possible they'd be trekking to Leah's brother's house on foot.

Returning to the trees, they stopped, mouths open. Elise spun in a slow circle, her face stunned.

The ropes that had tied Langor to the tree had been cut and were lying on the ground.

Hudson Langor had escaped.

"How did he escape?"

Elise was incredulous. Had Hudson had a knife with him?

"I doubt he was carrying a knife. I searched him pretty carefully."

Oh. She hadn't realized she'd been thinking out loud.

"So what does that mean? Someone assisted him?" She pursed her lips. It was the only thing that made sense to her.

"Looks like." Ryan removed his baseball cap and rubbed his head. That frown would carve out some permanent wrinkles soon, the way these past few days had gone. Whirling around, he stalked a few feet away, staring at the ground like it would give him some clues. "My question is, who would help him? And if he had more manpower, why didn't they attack us before we tied him up?"

"Um…maybe it was only one person? And you do have a gun."

A sudden smile broke through his somber expression. *Wow.* She blinked. She could stare at that face for the rest of her life.

Wait—what? No way was she following that thought.

Ryan strode to where she stood and put his hands on her shoulders. "Whatever his reason, I can't deny that I am happy we avoided another attack. Although I'm not happy that Hudson is on the loose again, I thought my heart would stop when he started waving that gun around earlier."

She reached out and touched his face. This was so not keeping her distance. She tried to remove her hand and found it trapped by his. For the briefest moment, her gaze was ensnared by his as he held her hand to his cheek.

Was he going to kiss her again? She thought he was. *Move, Elise.* But she didn't. Instead, she remained where she was, caught in the thrall of breathless fascination as he drew closer.

Who knows what might have happened. Before anything could, they were startled apart by the sound of an approaching motor. By the time the police cruiser rounded the bend, they were standing a discreet distance apart, facing the road. Did they both look as guilty as she felt? She gave Ryan an unobtrusive peek. His face showed nothing. His stance was casual. His ears, however, were a tad red.

A second cruiser pulled up behind the first. This time it was a LaMar Pond cruiser.

"Jackson!" Ryan grinned at his friend.

"Hey, Parker. Elise." Jackson tossed his own jaunty grin their way. "What do ya know?"

The New Wilmington officer joined them. "Sergeant Parker. Miss St. Clair. Are we missing something? I was sure I had heard you had a prisoner."

"Yeah, well, that's a story."

Elise bit the inside of her cheeks to keep from laughing at the way Ryan scrunched his face into a chagrined expression. He gave the two other officers a quick rundown of the events since they'd arrived in New Wilmington. When he reached the part about Langor holding the gun on Faith, the smiles on their faces vanished in an instant.

"Is she all right?" Jackson burst out.

"Where is she now?" the local officer demanded.

Holding up his hands, Ryan gave a slight shake of his head. "I'm getting there. She and her brother are the ones who called you from town. Then they headed back home. Neither of them wanted to press charges. I let them go." He turned to the New Wilmington cop. "I figured if you had a procedure you wanted to follow for interacting with the Amish, that was up to your department."

Ryan continued his story. The temptation to laugh struck again at Jackson's comical expression when Ryan explained how they'd come back to find Hudson gone. Maybe she was hysterical. There was nothing remotely humorous about the situation. A dangerous man, one who wanted to kill her and take her child, was on the loose. He would come back for her. She was sure of it.

All desire to laugh fled.

He would come back.

"What do you think, Elise?"

"Huh?" She'd been so deep in her thoughts, she'd completely missed Ryan's question.

"Jackson and Steele here," he said, indicating the local officer, "have offered to help us in our search for Leah, and for Langor. Jackson will go with us to the Byler residence. Steele is going to start combing the area for your brother-in-law."

"That sounds like a good plan."

"I'm going to radio in for backup." Officer Steele tipped his hat at her. She was reminded of a cowboy. He sauntered off in the direction of his cruiser, already talking into the radio hooked on his shoulder.

"Okey-doke." Jackson smacked his hands together, then rubbed them like a Boy Scout trying to start a fire with a stick. "Let's get this show on the road, what say you?"

"Sounds good."

Ryan moved ahead of his friend and opened the back door for Elise.

"I feel like a criminal," she muttered, folding herself into the back `seat.

"Sorry, sweetheart," Ryan sympathized, although his lips quirked in his signature crooked half smile. "There isn't room for all three of us up front."

As he shut the door and began to move away, she caught Jackson's raised eyebrows. *Sweetheart?* He mouthed the word to Ryan. She watched as he put his hand on Ryan's shoulder and said something else, no doubt teasing his friend as a tide of red swept past Ryan's collar. She chuckled as her cop swatted Jackson away to get into the car.

Her cop? Since when was Ryan Parker "her" anything? Sure, he'd kissed her. And her heart raced when he was near. But that didn't mean anything. She already knew that they didn't have a future.

Just thinking about it hurt. One more piece of her heart broke off inside. Even if they managed to rescue Mikey and Leah, and all the bad guys were stopped, she wouldn't be whole inside.

Staring at the back of Ryan's head as they drove toward Leah's family home, Elise ached.

She'd done it again. She'd given her heart to a man that she could never have.

Except this time, she didn't think she'd be able to heal.

FOURTEEN

Something was bothering Elise. Something more than just the strain of the past few days—which would be enough to knock anyone off their stride. No. Something troubling was going on inside her beautiful head since they'd met up with Jackson.

Was it the way Jackson had been teasing him? Did she think that they were making fun of her?

Nah. He discarded that idea immediately. Elise wasn't one to let a little teasing bring her down. If anything, she'd be right at home giving them a set-down.

Jackson pulled off onto a narrow road. After a long field, they came to a white farmhouse. The light blue door was faded. Just behind it, they could see the *dawdi haus*. That's where Leah's parents would have moved after their son got married. Along the side of the main house, a long clothesline ran the length of the building. It was full of dresses, trousers and shirts swaying in the gentle breeze. The sight sure was a different story from the night before. Except for two downed trees near the road, one wouldn't know that it had stormed so hard last night.

Jackson's cruiser splashed slowly through a couple of puddles as he maneuvered it behind the house. He took a minute to turn the vehicle around. Smart idea. If they needed to leave in a hurry, they didn't want to be slowed down by the car facing the wrong way.

Exiting the cruiser, the trio started toward the door. A slender woman was standing inside the door, watching their progress and drying her hands on a dish towel. She must have been doing dishes when they'd arrived. It was hard to tell what she thought of their presence. Although her brow was creased, Ryan was of the opinion that it was more from curiosity than dismay or distrust.

They stopped before the door. Jackson positioned himself just behind Ryan's shoulder, making it clear that this was Ryan's ball game. Technically, Jackson had more seniority, since he'd joined the force a year before Ryan himself did. It was the sign of a true friend that he seemed to understand how important this particular case was to Ryan.

Ryan didn't allow himself the luxury of wondering *why* this case was so important to him. He just acknowledged that his motivation to resolve this case was beyond making his father proud now.

"Mrs. Byler?" he addressed the woman.

"*Jah.* I am Lucy Byler." She didn't offer anything more.

"Ma'am, we were wondering if your husband was home?"

She finished drying her hands and motioned to a building across the street. "He is in there, working."

Thanking the woman for her time, they walked toward the building, which they could see was a furniture shop. Ryan marveled at the craftsmanship on the wooden benches and porch swings they passed. Inside the building, the sound of something scraping and voices conversing in German mingled.

The environment they stepped into was unlike other businesses. There was no music playing, no air-conditioning, and no computer screens or televisions on the wall. The two men inside were lifting benches onto a wagon. They stopped their conversation to watch the visitors approach. Jackson got the most attention, possibly because he was the one in a police uniform.

"Mr. Byler?" Ryan stopped before the two men. Which one was Leah's brother?

The younger man stepped forward, although his gaze was wary. "Abram Byler is me."

"Mr. Byler, I am Sergeant Parker, from the LaMar Pond Police Department." Was it his imagination or did the man tense at the name of LaMar Pond? "This is Sergeant Jackson and Elise St. Clair."

"St. Clair!" The man shifted his attention to Elise. He had definitely tensed now. "My sister, Leah, cleans for a Miss St. Clair."

"That's me."

He encountered her gaze, then looked at Ryan in confusion. Sensing his question, Ryan continued.

"Sir, have you seen your sister in the past week?"

"*Nee.* She is still at my cousin's." Now the man's gaze was concerned as it swung between Elise and Ryan.

He had to step carefully. "No, sir, I'm sorry to tell you that she's not. Several days ago, Leah left Miss St. Clair's home with a small child, a boy of three."

At Abram's exclamation, he continued quickly. "Her intent, we believe, was to save the child from harm. There is a man who is trying to find the boy and kidnap him. He is violent man, Mr. Byler, and your sister is still in danger. We have come to find Leah so that we can protect her and bring the boy home to his aunt." He pointed to Elise. "We are also working to make sure that the man is caught before he can harm Leah or anyone else."

Abram said something in Pennsylvania Dutch to his companion. The other man nodded and walked outside.

"Please. Come and sit." Abram led them to some benches along the wall. Uncomfortable, Ryan did as instructed. He much preferred to stand. It was with great effort that he sat still. Elise, he noticed, didn't even try. She sat on the edge of her seat and let one of her long legs bounce in her agitation. He could only sympathize.

"I have not seen my sister in several weeks. Are you sure she's heading home?"

Ryan returned his attention to the Amish man.

"She was spotted close to here yesterday, sir. And she still had the boy with her. It is our understanding that she was heading home under the belief that this would be the safest place for the two of them. Would you disagree?"

Abram rubbed at his beard. "Well, now, that may be so. Leah was right upset after our *mam* and *dat* passed. Seeing the *dawdi haus* empty was hard. She went to stay with my cousin, planning to come home before Christmas, when her grief had settled."

He stopped and quiet descended. Ryan waited to

see if he would continue to speak. When he didn't, Ryan broke the silence.

"We want to stay in the area and continue our search."

"You are welcome to remain with us tonight," Abram offered. "Tomorrow morning is church."

He'd heard about the Amish church practices. All the families in the district gathered at a different house every two weeks for a church service. Ryan was torn. Twenty families at one time would make it easier to ask around for Leah. On the other hand, the chance that someone else could get injured if Langor showed up was a concern.

"We will go to another *haus* for worship."

"Would your sister likely go to that house?"

"Leah would not know which *haus* we are at. She would come here."

At Abram's words, Ryan heaved a sigh of relief. "That will be good. If this man is nearby, I would hate for him to interrupt your services."

But Abram was looking perturbed. "If my sister is coming home—"

"If your sister is coming home, Mr. Byler, we will be here to get her to safety. It would be best if you didn't change your plans. But you could help your sister out. Ask around to see if anyone has seen Leah."

"I can do that."

It was agreed they would stay. After dinner, Jackson followed Ryan outside.

"What's going on with you and Elise?"

He kept his face turned away. "What do you mean?"

Jackson scoffed. "I'm not blind, dude. You two

keep giving each other goo-goo eyes. And then I heard you calling her *sweetheart*. And don't think I'm gonna believe that meant nothing. I know you. You never call any female older than five *sweetheart*."

He smiled at Jackson. How could he deny it to his friend? He was falling in love, in spite of himself, and unsure what to do about it. He wasn't even certain she felt the same way. "I don't know what's going on yet. But I'm hoping to find out."

"So am I to guess that white picket fences and babies may be in your future?"

He laughed. Jackson sounded horrified by the very idea. "Like I said, I don't know. But I think I would make a good dad."

Jackson sighed and shook his head mournfully. Then he laughed and shoved Ryan's shoulder. Grinning, Ryan shoved it back. It was a good night.

It was one of the longest days Elise could ever remember. Knowing that Mikey and Leah were nearby, but also knowing that Hudson, and possibly even that Dellon creep, were on the prowl for them, strained every last nerve to the breaking point.

Ryan and Jackson both took turns walking the perimeter, searching out any little sound, on the chance that Leah—or someone more dangerous—had arrived on the property. Elise herself couldn't stay away from the windows. She had balked when the men had declared she should stay inside the house. It went against the grain to hide, but in the end, she gave up. Mostly because, well, they were right. And also, because she saw how her being out in the open was distracting Ryan. She blushed, a little mortified at herself for arguing with him. If he needed her to stay inside so that he could focus his attention on finding Mikey and Leah, then she would stay inside. It was that simple.

Then she'd heard that conversation last night between Jackson and Ryan. And cried herself to sleep. Ryan would make a good dad. Too bad she couldn't have children.

After a restless night, Elise awoke to the sound of the buggy leaving the driveway—most likely the Bylers heading to church. Elise wandered into the kitchen to find a light breakfast waiting for her. Had Ryan and Jackson eaten yet? Their voices were coming from outside the back door.

After grabbing an apple, she bit into it as she went to find the two men. They both smiled at her as she exited the house. She moved to stand beside Ryan. He nodded at her, continuing to listen to Jackson talk. Elise tried to pay attention, but was soon distracted when Ryan reached across her back to rub her opposite shoulder blade. She didn't think he was even aware of his actions. Jackson was, though. She could see him biting back a grin.

They were discussing Dellon.

"I think I will take a drive to where the caller said he was spotted, see if I can learn anything. If he's still in the area, maybe I can nab him before he does any more harm, eh?" Jackson said.

"Hmm." Ryan looked across the yard. "I think, if you two agree, that Elise and I will stay here. I wouldn't want Leah to show up with no one here."

"Ryan." She tugged gently at his shirtsleeve. When he turned his eyes on her, she momentarily lost her train of thought. Getting it back, she forced herself to focus on the conversation. This was too important to let her mind wander. "Ryan, do you really believe Leah will head here? I mean, I would think she'd be leery of bringing trouble to her brother's doorstep."

"I hear what you're saying. But I still think this is where she'll come. I really do. She has to be growing desperate for a safe haven. She's trying to protect a child. And, Elise, remember, I know that she seems very mature, but she's still a teenager. If you were frightened and alone, wouldn't you want to go to the place where you knew someone loved you?"

That hit her hard, but she didn't flinch. At least not on the outside. On the inside, she felt as though his innocent words had pierced her. Because she didn't really have any place to go where she was loved. Not anymore. But Leah did. And listening to Ryan's reasoning, she had to admit it made sense.

"You're probably right." She tried to smile at him. He raised an eyebrow. She obviously wasn't as great at acting as she wanted to be. No matter. As soon as she had Mikey back, her life could go back to being normal. Just the way she liked it.

Liar.

She chose to ignore the small voice in her head. It did no good to dwell on her situation. It was what it was. She had to deal with it and move on.

Easier said than done.

Within ten minutes, Jackson had departed. Elise had expected that Ryan would immediately leave her to continue his search of the property. She was therefore startled when he followed her inside.

"Yes?" she asked. "Was there something you

needed?" She deliberately kept her voice aloof. She needed to start the separation now.

He looked a little hurt by her tone, and she was ashamed. But she couldn't back down. It was for his sake, as well as hers. Especially after last night.

She saw the moment when determination struck. Ryan's brow lowered and he stalked toward her. "I don't know why you're putting this wall between us. But when this is over, we're going to have a chat."

Spinning on his heel, he stalked off again.

Deflated, she sank down into a chair. But she didn't stay there for long. Last night, Ryan had found an old pair of binoculars in Jackson's car and had left them sitting on the table. Bored, and feeling broody, she picked up the binoculars and looked out the window. It was amazing how far away she could see with them.

She allowed her enhanced gaze to roam the horizon.

Then she jerked it back.

There. Out of the window, way off in the distance she saw something off. There it was again.

Rushing outside, she yelled for Ryan. When he came running, she grabbed on to his arms to steady herself. "Ryan," she gasped, hardly able to speak. "I was using these binoculars, and I saw someone hiding in the woods over there." She pointed. "I could be wrong, but I think it's Leah!"

FIFTEEN

Could they possibly move any slower?

Ryan had taken Elise seriously, but he'd also insisted on caution. Even if she had seen someone, they didn't know for sure it was Leah. It could have been anyone. And there had already been too many brushes with danger for them to run over there and land themselves in the middle of an ambush.

It took them almost an hour to hike to where Elise had thought she'd seen Leah. And to make matters worse, in her hurry to get over there, she'd twisted her ankle when she'd stepped into a hole hidden in the dirt. Her heart dropped the closer they got without seeing anyone. On the edge of the woods was an abandoned barn. They started to walk past it.

"Auntie Lise!"

Elise spun around so fast she nearly lost her balance.

"Mikey!"

Elise sobbed as the whirlwind that was her nephew dashed out of the barn and threw himself into her arms. His little arms wrapped around her neck so hard she was half strangled. She didn't care. It seemed like forever since her baby had been in her arms. For the moment, she forgot about everything except the joy of having him with her again as she cradled him close. He was dirty and didn't smell so sweet, but she didn't care.

"Mikey, are you okay? Are you hurt anywhere?" She couldn't move her head far enough away from him to check on his condition for herself.

He sniffled. "Not hurt. Hungry. Auntie Lise, I was scared. But I tried not to cry. I was a big boy."

Her heart ached. What had her baby been through? Still, she tried to inject cheer and calm into her response. "I'm glad that you were a big boy. I'm sure that helped Leah to take care of you."

Through the tears that tumbled down her cheeks, blurring her vision, she saw another figure draw closer. Blinking, Leah came into focus. Her dress was stained, and one of the sleeves was torn. Leah's cheeks were scratched. Even her bonnet showed signs of the hard journey she'd been on. Elise's heart overflowed with gratitude for the girl's bravery.

"Thank you," she choked out. "Thank you for protecting him."

Leah smiled faintly. It was the weariest smile she'd ever seen.

"Miss Byler, I'm Sergeant Parker." Ryan stepped up beside Elise, so close that their shoulders touched. Without thinking about it, Elise leaned into him. He readjusted his posture so that his arm was around her, supporting her. Mikey laid his head down on her shoulder, still clinging tightly. Ryan continued speaking to Leah. "Can you tell me what happened?"

Elise became aware that her ankle was smarting

again. Not wanting to miss any of the explanation, she was relieved to see that there was a bench near the barn wall. Sighing, she adjusted Mikey in her arms and moved to sit down on the bench. Hopefully, it was sound enough to hold their weight. Leah walked over and sat beside her. Ryan remained standing, although he did move closer.

"I was at your house to clean," Leah said, addressing Elise. "I knew that your babysitter was supposed to be there, but she didn't open the door for me. I thought maybe she was on the phone, or maybe she was asleep."

She looked at Elise. Not knowing what she was supposed to say, Elise just nodded for her to continue.

"I went into the living room, and that's when I saw her. I thought she was dead. I called you."

"Yeah." Elise cleared her throat, shuddering as she recalled the phone call that had started everything.

"I heard noises. I thought someone was still in the house. I thought, I need to get Mikey. I need to protect him, *jah*? I went into his room and I found him, and I woke him up. There were footsteps in the house. I told Mikey we were going to play a game, and we climbed out a window. When we were in the trees, I looked back. I could see a very large man on the porch."

Hudson.

"He had on a white shirt, but there was a red stain on his shirt. I thought, there's blood on his shirt. The dead woman's blood." She buried her face in her hands for a second. They waited, for clearly she needed a minute to compose herself.

"I didn't know what to do. I was so scared. Then he started yelling out Mikey's name. I was afraid he'd hurt him. I started going to my cousin's house, but when I got there, I saw men had come, and I heard them asking about me and a boy. I knew it wasn't safe there, so I decided to come here. I found a friend who drove me partway, then we walked."

Amazed at the young girl's quick thinking, Elise again was overcome by gratitude. There was no doubt in her mind that Leah had saved Mikey from being taken.

"But, Leah, why didn't you go the rest of the way home?" she asked. "Why stay out here in the woods? Didn't you think your family would help you?"

"*Jah*, I knew that Abram would help me. He's a *gut* brother. Strong, and he would protect me. But I got scared again. I was close to his house. A car drove past. We were in the woods, I don't think they saw us."

"Who, Leah? Who was it?" Her stomach hurt.

Leah's face was so pale it was astonishing to Elise that she hadn't passed out. "The men. The men who went to my cousin's *haus*. They were here. They drove past three times."

A tear dripped off her chin onto the apron over her blue dress. "I didn't know what to do. I was close to my home. I could hear my brother's voice as he worked. But I could not go home. I was afraid the men would hurt my brother or his wife if I went to them."

Elise couldn't tell her she was wrong. In fact, she suspected that Leah had actually saved her brother's life by not going home. If Dellon was bold enough to keep driving by her house, he obviously expected her to show up sooner or later. How long would it be until he showed up again?

She looked at Ryan for guidance.

Intercepting her glance, he nodded and then began to speak.

"Leah, I have a friend in New Wilmington. He's a police officer, like me. He is checking out something at the moment. When he returns, I want to take you and Mikey and Elise back to the police station."

Watching him, she felt pride in what he did, how seriously he took his position. She had been right to tell him that he was meant to be a police officer. Every move he made showed how determined he was to see that the innocent were protected and that justice was done.

When no protest came from the ladies, Ryan continued. "Once the three of you are secure, I plan to come back here. I need to stop Leroy Dellon and Hudson Langor, for one. And I need to make sure that your family is safe. When all this is over, Leah, I know that your brother will be happy to have you home."

A thought occurred to Elise. "Ryan, I am wondering if there were any clues in either Dellon's house or van about why he is chasing us?"

He looked at her with an approving smile. "Nothing we found pointed directly to you. But I strongly suspect that Hudson is the reason—because of his connection to you and your nephew. Whether Hudson instigated the whole thing, I don't know. I keep going back to what he said about his boss trying to kill him. Was that Dellon, or was he working with another criminal, too? Who put the hit on him? I don't like all these loose ends."

How on earth was she ever going to find peace with such evil surrounding her? Was it even possible to stop all the people after her? She'd done her best to live a good life, to raise her nephew to be a kind and polite child. And this is what happened.

Was it worth it?

Mikey snuggled deeper into her shoulder. She kissed his head again. Yes, it was worth it. She had no idea why God was letting her go through this trial. But she reminded herself that He hadn't left her. She wasn't alone.

Her vison moved to include Ryan. No, she wasn't alone. God had known that she would need help. And He'd sent her someone capable of shouldering her burdens with her for a time. In her heart, she wished it could be for a lifetime. She could almost convince herself it didn't matter that she couldn't have children. She was fairly sure that he felt as strongly for her as she did for him.

Her thoughts flashed back to the conversation he'd had with Jackson. He was a good man. How could she deny him the opportunity for a family, knowing that he longed for one?

She straightened her shoulders. She wouldn't be selfish. She'd accept his help in the current situation. Then she'd move on.

She sat quietly, holding her sweet boy as her heart shattered inside her.

Ryan paced back in forth in front of the barn, frustration making him cagey. He couldn't understand what was going on inside Elise's head. For the past forty-five minutes, she'd been quietly talking with Leah. He'd tried to catch her attention several times, but she never looked his way.

He couldn't help feeling that she was ignoring

him. Why? To the best of his knowledge, he hadn't done anything. Well, anything except for working like crazy to save her life and find Mikey. But besides that...

He bit back a groan. Now he was getting petty. Seriously, though, he had woken up this morning feeling refreshed and eager to start his day. More to the point, he had been eager to see her. The desire to tell her how he felt was so strong he was ready to explode with it.

And then she'd gotten up and completely shut him down. Oh, sure, she was polite, and a time or two he thought he'd detected a chink in the wall she'd built up around herself. But before he could talk with her about his feelings, she'd hidden behind it again.

Now she was deliberately ignoring all his attempts to get her attention. He knew that if he told her it was something important, something related to the case, she'd listen and do what he instructed. On that front, they were in sync with each other. Personal feelings, though, were another matter.

What was he to do?

Leave it alone, Ryan. Get her home, make sure she and Mikey are safe. Then you can work out any issues.

If she let him. What if she didn't want anything to do with him once the case was over?

He didn't even want to go there.

A lone car drove down the road. Ryan stopped pacing and ducked deeper inside the barn. He couldn't see it too well from where he stood because of the distance. All he could tell was that it was a maroon sedan.

"Elise," he hissed.

She looked up at him, startled. It was proof of how

serious the situation was that he didn't say anything snarky about her finally looking at him.

"Where are those binoculars?"

Without questioning, she set Mikey down and hurried over, her arm outstretched to hand them to him. As he took them, their fingers brushed. Just barely, but enough for a sharp spark of electricity to dance between them. Elise flinched.

He ignored it. Now was definitely not the time.

Raising the binoculars to his eyes, he adjusted them until the scene in front of him cleared. The sedan loomed like it was two feet away. His heartbeat kicked up. There, right in the driver's seat, sat Leroy Dellon. His head was turned toward the Byler home, away from the woods, but Ryan knew it was him. He didn't have anyone in the car with him. Where had the rest of his goons gone? And how had he gotten the vehicle? Stolen, most likely. Unease trickled down Ryan's spine. He hoped that the criminal boss hadn't gotten the vehicle by killing someone. He had a bad feeling that he had done just that.

Dellon turned his head and looked straight at Ryan. Ryan jumped back, his stomach dropping. Wait. They were far enough away that Dellon shouldn't have been able to see inside the barn. He puffed out his cheeks and exhaled the air in his lungs, fast.

Man, for a moment, he'd thought they were caught.

When would Jackson return? The sooner he got back, the sooner they could move out.

A little hand tugged at his jeans leg. Mikey was trying to get his attention. He sure was a cute little guy.

"Hi, kiddo. What's up?" He ruffled the boy's curly brown hair. He had the same hazel eyes as his aunt.

"Are you a friend of Auntie Lise?"

That was a good question. Was he? "Sure, I'm her friend."

The little boy grinned. "Cool. I wanna be a cop when I get big."

Aw, this kid was just melting his heart. "Do you? Have you told your auntie that?"

The dark head shook. No. That would be an interesting conversation to watch. Not that Ryan expected her to be upset. He imagined it would just be a serious conversation where she'd say that she was proud of him for wanting to help others. The kind of conversation that should happen in a family.

A family that he wanted to be a part of.

"Well, well, well. Isn't this a cozy gathering?" a cold voice sneered from the doorway.

Ryan turned. Two of Dellon's henchmen crowded in the doorway, guns pointed right at their small group. Angered with himself for becoming distracted, Ryan wondered if he could get his hands on his gun fast enough to fight back. He quickly discarded that idea. By the time he'd pulled the service weapon out, the men would have had time to shoot at least one, and most likely more, of their small group. He'd best wait for an opportunity to strike.

Mikey began to cry.

"Quiet, brat!" one of them growled at the child, moving his arm back as if to strike him.

Reacting fast, Ryan shoved Mikey out of arm's reach and towards his aunt. Elise caught the child by his shirt and pulled him the rest of the way to her, placing her body between the child and the strangers.

One of them laughed. "It don't matter. You'll be coming with us."

"What about this one?" The second man shrugged a shoulder toward Ryan. "Should we kill 'im?" The eagerness that lit his face made Ryan's stomach turn. He'd always known getting killed in the line of duty was a possibility, but he was far from ready to die.

The other guy, however, stared at his companion like he'd lost his mind. "Are you nuts? You know how hard they'd look for us for killin' a cop? I plan on enjoying the money I get for this job. Not hiding because some moron I work with decided to off a cop."

Amazing. Scruples in a hired killer. Who'd have thought?

"That don't mean we can't do this." The man reached out, lightning quick, and struck out with his gun. Ryan jerked his arm up to protect himself. Elise screamed. The gun connected with his head and he crumpled.

Ryan had no idea how long he'd been out.

Jumping to his feet, he tried to ignore the stabbing pain in his skull. He staggered outside of the barn. In the distance he could hear voices. Good. They hadn't gone too far. Which meant he'd only been out for a couple of minutes.

He ran as fast as his aching head would allow. It seemed to take forever until he saw them beyond the tree line.

Mikey cried out as he was pushed into a car. He could see that Leah was already inside. Why were they taking her? Though he wished he could have gotten her to safety, he had to admit he was relieved the thugs hadn't simply killed the girl once she wasn't needed anymore.

Elise was forced into the car next. When she struggled, the man closest to her slammed a meaty fist into her jaw. She crumpled. Rage filled Ryan as he continued running until he reached the street.

The second man, the one who'd wanted to kill him in the barn, saw him coming and took aim. Ryan dove to the ground as the shot exploded from the gun. Hearing the car door slam and the engine rev, Ryan jumped to his feet again and ran toward the car, his own weapon out.

He had to stop them.

Holding his gun steady, he shot at the tire. It popped with a loud hiss of air. The car swerved but didn't stop. Revving up, it headed straight for him. He couldn't risk another shot at this distance. It might go wild and hit Elise, Leah or Mikey.

The car was upon him. At the last moment, he tried to leap out of the way. Unfortunately, his reflexes were slow from the blow he'd taken to his head. As he jumped to the side, the car clipped him, and he was tossed in the air. The last thing he heard before slamming to the ground was Elise screaming his name.

Then blackness swallowed him again.

SIXTEEN

Mikey was crying.

Elise became aware of his sobs, coming as if from a distance. Her eyelids were like lead weights over her eyes. With a grunt, she forced herself to lift them. It was so difficult. Her vision wavered. Blinking, she worked to clear up her eyesight.

As she slowly came awake, she realized that something heavy was leaning against her side. She was lying down, her hands down at her sides. Her muscles were cramped. She was on the floor. But on the floor where?

Lifting her head as far as she was able, she saw Mikey lying against her, crying. She dragged her hand over to him and touched his arm. He jolted into a sitting position. The tears had made tracks down his dirty face. His mouth trembled. Her poor baby. Her gaze searched him. He didn't look hurt. Just scared.

"Auntie Lise. I thought you was dead. Like my mommy. You wouldn't wake up." His little voice broke into sobs at the last word.

"Shush, Mikey. I'm okay." She took a mental inventory of herself. Other than the heavy, slightly woozy feeling, she seemed to be in one piece. Nothing hurt, other than her head. But for how long would that stay the case? As happy as she was to be alive, she could hardly believe it. It seemed to her that it would have made more sense for Hudson or that Leroy fellow to finish her off. She still wasn't sure what was going on. But it was obvious that there was no love lost between the two men, neither of whom was in the room.

Leah! What had they done with the Amish girl? She didn't remember anything after being hit on the head.

Elise struggled to a half-sitting position. Now she had a clear view of her surroundings. Hardwood floors. A large open room with neatly spaced wooden benches. No television. No phone or computer. Simple wooden furniture. Through the window, she could see a clothesline stretching out from the side of the house. No pictures with family members hung on the walls.

She was certain they were in an Amish house. Was it the Byler home? Leah's family's house? Her gut clenched as a wave of nausea rolled over her. Where was Leah's family? Where was Leah?

Dread shivered up her spine.

Please, Lord. Let them be alive. Let us survive this. Then she remembered.

Ryan. He'd been run over! She had been so afraid when the one man had struck him with his gun. She'd never seen anyone collapse so hard. Never would she forget the sound his body had made as it hit the ground. Her relief when he'd run after them had been short-lived. When the car had struck him, she knew he wouldn't be getting up again. Her stomach heaved. It was all she could do to keep herself from vomiting.

Grief swamped her, pulling her down. She couldn't believe he was dead. Those thugs had killed the man she loved. Even though she knew she could never be the woman for Ryan, she would have had the comfort of knowing he was still alive, doing a job he loved. Now…

A sob escaped through the hard knot clogging her throat, choking her.

"Auntie Lise?" Mikey's frightened voice drew her.

"It's okay, baby." She pulled him close, inhaling his little-boy scent. Her baby needed a bath, but he was warm and, for the moment, safe. She had to stay strong for his sake. No matter what happened to her, he would survive if she could make it happen.

Heavy, running steps announced that they weren't alone anymore. She waited. Would it be Hudson, come to finish what he started?

She turned to glare. Only it wasn't Hudson who entered the room. It was Leroy Dellon, the man who'd put out a contract on her, though she was still unsure why. He glared at her, malevolence emanating from him like a strong cologne. She pulled Mikey back, pushing her boy behind her. The man staring at her sneered.

"Do you really believe that you'll be strong enough to protect him?" He sat on a bench across from her, then spat on the floor, a dark tobacco-filled stream that left an ugly stain on the polished floors. It reminded her of evil, leaving a dark stain on his soul. Then he spoke again. "Make no mistake, Miss St. Clair. You're alive for one reason. Bait. You and the boy lured Langor out of hiding. The fool. For a time, I thought I'd successfully killed him. If he'd stayed hidden, I wouldn't have known otherwise. He's been disappointing. I expected more loyalty from him." He said it almost sadly. Then he flashed her a smile that made her shudder. "I think you'll be the method that I use to make Langor pay for his betrayal."

What? Did they honestly think she was in league with Hudson? If he'd been watching and listening, surely he knew that she feared Hudson.

"I don't know anything! He killed my sister. I would never help him!"

He laughed. It was not a pleasant sound. "Young lady, it really doesn't matter what lies you say to cover your tracks now. You had to know something. You were staying in his house when your sister, his wife, went to the police with information."

Her head reared back. "My sister never made it to the police!"

He gave her that horrible soul-chilling smile again. "She did. Unfortunately for her, her contact was working for me. The SD card that Langor has been searching for is in my possession. That sealed her fate. What sealed his is that she called my informant later and said she had more evidence. Evidence that proved Langor had been working on a specific job. For a specific person. Me. I couldn't let her live. Nor could I let him get away with gathering information to use against me. That's why she had to be eliminated."

Elise felt as though she was watching a weird movie where the sound and picture weren't synced. As hard as she tried, she couldn't quite make out what was happening. What was he saying?

"Hudson killed my sister!"

He shook his head, an ugly grin stretching across

his face. His eyes were so cold she shivered in response. "No. He was ordered to kill her after our mole in the police department reported what she'd done, but he balked. I had generously given him a way to prove he was loyal and he failed. He was making plans to hide the woman and the kid. He forgot how careful I am. It never occurred to him that he was being watched. We couldn't let her get away, and he needed to be taught a lesson. He walked in after she was dead. Once that happened, he thought he'd hide from us, but we followed him. He's gonna have to pay a little for his betrayal. And the key to his punishment is right there." He jerked his head at the child clinging to Elise's side.

"No! He's just a baby! He has no part in this."

Leroy Dellon sent a bored look her way. "Do I look like I care? You and that kid are the only things that Langor has left."

Now she understood. She was still alive because they thought that she could be forced to reveal what Karalynne had told their mole she'd found that implicated Dellon. But Elise didn't know anything. Her sister had never shared that she'd found anything else.

Another thought struck her. Leah's family. What had happened to them? She had no idea how long she'd been out. Had they come home already, or were they still at church?

"Did you kill the people that live here?" She forced the words from her tight throat. She'd never forgive herself if she'd been responsible for their deaths. Not that it looked like she'd live that much longer herself. *Stop it!* She couldn't afford to give up.

An image of Ryan came to her mind, but she

tamped it down, deep inside. If she let herself think of how she'd never see him again, she knew the grief would be her undoing. And she had to get Mikey through this situation. Even if she herself didn't make it out, he had to live.

A harsh laugh interrupted her thoughts. "The family isn't here. She said it was a church Sunday." He jerked his thumb toward a darkened corner. For the first time, Elise noticed Leah crumpled in the corner. There was blood on the side of her face. She'd apparently been struck. Elise's heart lurched when Leah slowly opened her eyes. They were dull with pain, but the Amish girl was alive. Elise averted her gaze. She doubted if Dellon knew she was awake. If that was true, she didn't want to be the one to alert him to that fact.

Elise heard a sudden crash a second before the door banged open, slamming into the wall and bouncing back with the force. Hudson Langor burst into the room, swinging a gun wildly.

"Dellon!" he roared.

Leroy Dellon had stood abruptly as Hudson entered. Now he sat back with a languid smile. The gun in his enemy's hands didn't seem to faze him at all.

Elise took the opportunity to scoot herself and Mikey farther away from the men.

"Uh-uh." Dellon swung his own gun in her direction. "It would be a shame to waste this opportunity, now that our friend Langor has arrived."

That's when Elise noticed what Hudson had missed. Another man had entered the room behind him. She didn't know who it was. What she did know was that her chances of surviving had just plummeted.

She said a quick prayer under her breath. Not for herself—for Mikey and Leah, the two innocents who'd been pulled into this mess.

"Parker! Parker, can you hear me?"

Parker opened his eyes and stared blearily at the oval shape shimmying in front of him. He blinked, and it coalesced into Jackson's face, paler than he'd ever seen him.

"Yeah, I'm good." Feeling ridiculous lying in the dirt, Ryan shoved himself to a sitting position. He couldn't quite stop the groan that emerged as his muscles protested, although he managed to cut it off before it got too embarrassing. He gave himself a brief once-over, stretching each muscle methodically. He wasn't dizzy or nauseous. Probably not a concussion, although how he had avoided that he didn't know.

His hip ached where the car had clipped him, but other than that, he seemed to be in good shape. Satisfied, he stood. Time was not his friend. How long had he been out?"

"What time is it?"

"About one."

An hour. He'd lost an hour. Who knew how far those thugs had gone with Elise, Leah and Mikey?

"Elise! And Mikey! We need to find them!" Was that his voice? He never barked like that. He didn't take the time to apologize. Not when the woman he loved was in danger.

He had never told her that he felt that way. The feelings had grown so quickly. But that didn't mean it wasn't true. He was in love with Elise, completely and without reservation. If he was right, she felt the same for him. He shrugged the knowledge back. He'd deal with it later. After he'd found them and made sure the danger was eliminated.

"Parker."

He focused on Jackson.

"We know where they are. A small band of men with guns were seen at the Byler farm. There are already cruisers on their way there."

The Byler farm. So Elise, Mikey and Leah were close by. Ryan rubbed his hand against his stomach, trying to knead out the knots. He couldn't relax, not knowing that so many things could go wrong.

"That's where we need to go." He set his jaw, fully expecting his friend to argue and tell him he needed to go to the hospital. To his surprise and relief, Jackson gave him a hard once-over, then nodded. Only the way his mouth tightened showed how much it went against the grain.

"Fine. Don't make me regret this, Parker. And once we get your girl and her nephew out of danger, just remember. You owe me. Big-time."

He didn't even bother to protest that Elise wasn't his girl. Because in his heart, she was.

"Absolutely." He stalked to Jackson's car and let himself into the passenger side, glad that they wouldn't have to hike back to the farm. It had taken almost an hour to hike out to the abandoned barn where they'd found Leah earlier. *Come on, Jackson. Get the lead out.* Jackson climbed in and started the vehicle, then sent Ryan an irritated glance. *What? Oh.* His hands were clenched into fists and he was pounding the right one against the top of the door. Bringing his fist back down to his leg, he forced himself to sit still. He was, after all, a sergeant in the LaMar Pond PD.

"Sorry." His voice was low.

"Parker, we'll get her back."

Ryan nodded in thanks. Inside, though, he was hollow. Jackson meant well, but no one could promise that. They could already be too late. He'd lost his best friend to violence once, but that pain wouldn't be nearly as bad as what he'd deal with if he lost Elise and her nephew.

Bowing his head, he did the only thing he could. *Please, Lord. Keep them safe. I give them over to Your care.*

Still, when the car pulled to a stop near the other cruisers on the edge of the farm, Ryan shot out of the car before Jackson had come to a full stop. He ignored Jackson's voice coming from inside the vehicle and hurried over to where the local chief stood directing the operation. The man nodded to him but didn't stop giving low-voiced commands into his radio.

"The family doesn't appear to be in the house, sir. And there is no evidence of a break-in."

"They must be in one of the other buildings, Jones. Check the barn. Take backup and don't take unnecessary chances."

The man on the other end agreed.

Parker's mind was busy with the implications. No bodies had been found. Some of the tension left him. Casting a glance around, he spotted several large motorcycles behind the barn. The sight was incongruous with the Amish surroundings. There was a single buggy in the side yard.

He was even more grateful now that the family had

left that morning. If only they could apprehend the criminals before the Bylers came home.

Sudden gunfire erupted from the barn.

Ryan's heart stopped.

All talking ceased.

A moment later, a police radio came to life. Jones's voice echoed in the air. "We have the situation under control, sir. Four men, one injured."

"What about the women and the child?" the team leader asked.

"No women or children here, sir. We're still searching for them. And none of these men are Dellon or Langor."

Ryan wanted to scream with frustration. The faces around him were grim, obviously concluding that the absences of the women and child meant that they'd been killed, and the bodies disposed of. A movement caught his eye. There was a smaller house standing apart from the main house. Almost behind it. And someone was moving around in it.

"There's someone in the *dawdi haus*," he murmured.

The team leader directed the men toward the house. Ryan didn't wait for the instructions. He joined them, as did Jackson. As the group moved closer, the officer in the lead motioned for them to separate and surround the building. Ryan and Jackson started around the back of the house. Two men burst out of the house, no doubt in response to the gunfire. They were quickly and quietly subdued. Dellon had more men than they'd thought.

The door was open. Approaching the door, he could hear angry male voices inside. Jackson dropped back.

Ryan could hear him telling the chief they were going in. Ryan didn't wait to hear if the officer in charge agreed or not.

A woman cried out. Elise. Ryan hurried forward, careful to stick close to the wall and step quietly. He listened to the conversation, his pulse pounding.

"So, Langor, you managed to get away. The others should have kept a better eye on you. You always were a slippery one. Now that you're here, at my mercy, it will give me great pleasure to watch you suffer for your betrayal."

"I didn't betray you. You betrayed me! Killing my wife and then trying to kill me."

A tsking sound. "Now, Hudson, old friend, none of that would have happened if your wife hadn't found out about us. That was your fault. You liked to brag a bit too much."

"But I didn't—" He huffed out an annoyed grunt. "It's not like you'll listen anyway. So fine. Great. It was my fault. Look, you can have the woman and the boy. I probably wouldn't get much for them anyway. If you have the card, then why don't we say we're even and go our separate ways?"

So that's why he wanted his son. Disgust welled up in Ryan. The man was planning on selling his own son. He truly was despicable. Ryan continued to inch forward. He could see just inside the doorway now. Two men were standing there. Both had guns. The second man had his gun pointed at Hudson. Ryan wanted to shoot, but he couldn't risk the civilians. And he knew that at least two of them, Elise and Mikey, were in that room.

"I don't think so. You need to pay for your arrogance." The first voice had lost its congeniality. It was cold now. The voice of a killer.

Without warning, Hudson Langor threw himself at one of the men, reaching for his gun. There was a scuffle. Then a gunshot. Leroy's henchman standing in the doorway moved to shoot. Ryan shot him instead. He fell, and Ryan rushed into the room. Two men were on the floor. The one on the bottom was struggling to shove off the still form lying on top of him. Elise was crouched off to the side, Mikey safely stowed behind her. In the corner, he could see Leah, but wasn't sure of her condition.

Jackson charged into the room, with two other officers. Within a minute, Hudson Langor was pulled off Leroy Dellon, who was uninjured. Hudson was alive, but he had been shot in the side. As soon as the villains were secured, Ryan went over to be sure that Elise and Mikey were well.

"We're fine." Elise briefly touched his face as she cradled her nephew in her arms. "It's Leah I'm worried about."

Ryan glanced at her again, reassuring himself, then moved over to Leah. A brief inspection told Ryan that Leah would be fine. She had been hit on the head but was otherwise uninjured. She'd pretended to be dead so as not to draw the man's attention. She agreed to let the paramedics look at her when they arrived.

Jackson joined him. Ryan let him take over with Leah and moved to where the woman he loved sat. He squatted down to her level. Her smoky hazel eyes, tired and teary, were the most gorgeous things he'd ever seen. He could breathe freely again, knowing she was well and Mikey was unharmed. He smiled when

Mikey started to squirm and Elise allowed the child to slide from her arms.

Reaching out, Ryan placed his hand along the curve of her cheek. The warmth of her skin was a healing balm to his aching heart.

As if his touch had awoken her, Elise exploded forward and threw her arms around Ryan's neck. Her hold was tight. She might strangle him, but he found he was too grateful to care. His eyes burned. He squeezed them shut, burying his face briefly in her hair, inhaling deeply.

Calmer, he gently set her back, then pulled Mikey toward him to embrace the scared little boy. "Hey, tiger. You okay?"

"I'm okay, Mr. Ryan. I was scared."

Another wave of emotion caught at his throat. He cleared it and blinked again. "I know. But you are okay. Both you and your aunt are fine."

"Ryan." Would he ever get tired of hearing her say his name?

"Yes, sweetheart?"

She blushed, but continued. "I didn't think I'd ever see you again."

Ryan couldn't help himself. He gathered Elise and Mikey near again. He'd come so close to losing them.

It didn't take long for him to realize something else was wrong. Elise had been happy to see him, he knew it. Even if she didn't say it, the hug she'd given him told him that her feelings for him were far from indifference. But that didn't stop her from pushing him away.

It wasn't anything that he could put his finger on. And yet, as the horrible day went on, he could feel the wall she'd built going back up between them. After they'd been checked for injuries and all the arrests had been made, Ryan watched Elise hug Leah tightly. Leah had decided against returning to LaMar Pond.

By the time the Byler family returned from church, the criminals had all been rounded up, Hudson was on his way to the hospital, accompanied by an officer, and Mikey had fallen asleep in the back of Jackson's cruiser.

"Will Hudson be okay?" Elise asked softly.

Ryan shrugged. "He'll heal from his injuries. He'll also spend the rest of his life in jail. He might not have killed your sister, but he's killed many others. I talked to the chief. The evidence your sister had found was at Dellon's place. There was actual footage of hits Langor had done."

"I think he was planning on selling Mikey. That's why he wanted him."

He wished he could comfort her and drive the grief from her eyes.

Ryan and Elise had gotten back into Jackson's car. When Jackson pulled into Elise's driveway, Ryan signaled to his friend that he wanted to talk with Elise alone. Jackson remained with the car while Ryan walked the woman who held his heart in her hands to the door. Mikey was still asleep and was slumped against her shoulder.

"Elise, are you sure you're okay?"

"Yes, Ryan. I'm fine."

Fine. Why was it that he never believed her when she said she was fine? Her voice had a flat quality to it. He didn't trust it.

"Honey—"

"Ryan, I'm sorry," she interrupted. She wouldn't meet his eyes. "I'm tired. This day…no, actually, the past *several* days have been a trial. I can barely think right now. Could we talk later? I really just want to go to sleep."

What could he say to that? Reluctantly, he said good-night, leaning forward to kiss Mikey on the top of his head. He kissed Elise softly on the cheek, then backed away.

"I'll call you," he promised. She nodded.

As he walked back to the car, he looked over his shoulder. She stood where he'd left her. Her shoulders seemed to be slumped, almost defeated. They should have been celebrating. They were alive, the danger had been resolved, Mikey was unharmed and Ryan's heart was ready to burst with his love for her.

Instead, it seemed some invisible chasm had opened between them.

SEVENTEEN

 W hy wasn't she returning his calls?

Ryan frowned as the now-familiar voice-mail message played. "Hi! You've reached Elise. I'm not available—"

He clicked the end button, not listening to the rest of the recording or leaving a message. What was the point? She hadn't responded the other six messages he'd left over the course of the past week. There was a very high probability that she wouldn't bother to answer this one, either. He'd just look pathetic. Or more pathetic than he already did. Six messages.

He clenched his teeth, glaring at the phone in his hand as if it was at fault for his current misery. Shoving the phone into his back pocket, he grabbed his sunglasses and keys off his desk and stood, stretching. His shift was over, the ten million forms the department required him to complete were done and his stomach was growling. Time to head home.

He didn't want to go home. Not yet. What he did want was to swing by and pick up Elise and Mikey and take them out to dinner. Or even better, bring dinner to them and have a quiet meal at her home. Like a family. He wanted that so badly, but it was obviously she didn't.

The ache he'd been ignoring for the past week intensified. There was a tightness in his chest, almost like he had a bad cold coming on. No medicine would heal him, either. What had he done to cause her to reject him?

If she wanted to let him know she wasn't interested now that the danger was past, couldn't she have just told him so? Leaving him hanging like this...

Home was not appealing right now. It would simply remind him that he was alone. Again. Glancing around, he saw that Willis was just coming in. Willis with his perfect family. Beautiful wife. Twin toddlers. And a new baby at home. He was talking to Tucker, who also had a family to go home to. Even the chief and Olsen were married now.

He liked them all. Considered them friends and enjoyed being around them. But, right now, he needed a little space. Decision made, he walked out, waving a brief farewell, pretending he didn't see the concern darkening Willis's face or the way Tucker cocked his head and frowned. *Nope. No reason to feel bad for me. Just because the woman I love wants nothing to do with me.*

Once outside, he slipped the sunglasses on and headed for his truck, without any real idea of where he was going.

"Parker! Yo!"

Ryan's head jerked up and glanced back. He'd been so deep in his own thoughts that he'd walked right past Jackson. The back of his neck heated up.

"Sorry, Jackson. I wasn't paying attention."

"Yeah, guess so." Jackson put his hands in his pockets and sauntered over. "So have you heard from Elise lately?"

Way to turn the knife, buddy. Only that wasn't Jackson's style. He was blunt, but he wasn't cruel. If he was asking, it was because he was concerned. Or knew something.

"Okay. Out with it. What do you know?"

Jackson raised his hands. "Now, don't get sharp, Parker. You know that I want you to be happy. And you have been moping around here something pitiful. What's going on?"

A sigh he hadn't even realized was there whooshed out of his lungs. "Nothing's going on. That's the problem. The woman won't return my calls. I haven't heard from her for a week. I stopped in at the 911 center and was told she'd taken some time off. I get that. I'd want a break, too, if I'd been through that. But to shut me out? Clearly, I misunderstood what was happening between us."

Jackson hesitated, which was unusual. "Okay. I know this isn't my place. I'm not good with the emotional stuff. I gotta ask, though…do you love her?"

"Yeah."

That one word hung in the thick summer air.

"Man, you can't just let her go. Talk to her. In person. You know where she lives."

True. But part of him hesitated. It would be easier to have his arm cut off than to have to hear her say she didn't love him and didn't want him around. He wiped a hand across his mouth, giving himself time.

"Hey, guys!" Lily called with her Chicago accent, approaching them. It was good to see her up and about. Today was her first day back on the job. "You guys having a party? Why wasn't I invited?" She flipped her short dark hair out of her eyes as she came to a stop before them.

"Hey, Lily. What do ya know?" Jackson gave his standard response.

She stared at Parker, a meaningful look in her eyes. "What I know is that I drove past Elise St. Clair's house this morning and there was a for-sale sign in the yard."

"What?" Ryan exploded. She was moving?

"You gotta go see her." Jackson put a hand on his shoulder. "Ryan. You'll never forgive yourself if you don't try before she leaves."

Ryan froze. The truth in those words struck deep. And more than that. He could sense the regret flavoring the tone. Jackson had experience with regret. Ryan had almost forgotten it. The other man was so good at playing casual.

"You're right. Thanks, guys. Say a prayer for me."

"Will do." Jackson nodded. Lily grimaced. Faith was a touchy subject with her. They'd have to keep working on that.

Right now, though, he needed to see his Elise and convince her to stay and give him a second chance. Give *them* another chance. Heart pounding with his new purpose, he got in his truck. When he pulled around the curve before her house, his gut clenched at the white-and-blue sign set up near the base of her driveway. He swallowed. *Lord, please help me to handle whatever happens.*

A few seconds later, he was driving up the long lane to her house.

He was glad he hadn't hesitated.

Elise's car was there. The trunk was wide-open, and there were already suitcases and boxes inside. Apparently, she wasn't waiting for the house to sell before she left. Slowly he left his truck and moved toward the car. Muffled strains of music drifted from the house. It was so soft he could barely hear it. It sounded like a lullaby. He could see some of Mikey's toys had already been stowed away. Would she really have left without telling him? Obviously. The proof was right in front of him.

The music grew louder briefly. Then the screen door slammed. Whipping his head around, he stepped away from the car as Elise marched around the corner, holding another box. She halted when she saw him, her hazel eyes widening. If her looks were anything to go on, the past week hadn't been easy on her, either. Dark purple smudges were under her eyes. Her shoulders were slightly slumped. *She looks so tired.* At that moment, Ryan forgot the anger that had started to build. All he wanted to do was go to her and take her in his arms, to comfort her and support her as a man in love should be able to do.

He couldn't do that, though he still didn't know why.

"Elise." Even her name was like a balm to his weary soul now that he saw her. If only he could touch her. Not yet. "What's going on?"

Lifting her chin, Elise's lips tightened. His own shoulders tensed in response.

"I think it's pretty clear what's happening." Her words sounded hard, but he caught the slight wobble.

She wasn't as sure of herself as she trying to appear. "I'm moving. I put my house up for sale—"

"Elise, please—just talk to me. I can't believe you would think I would be okay with you leaving like this, without even an explanation." Okay, now he was starting to sound too emotional. He couldn't seem to stem the words, though. They'd been brewing all week. "I thought we had something growing between us. I thought that we had become friends, and more. Close enough for you to return my calls. Instead, I hear from someone else that your house is for sale. You were going to leave without even saying good-bye to me? Did I mean nothing to you? You couldn't even tell me yourself that you wanted nothing to do with me?"

His last words erupted in a strident tone, almost a shout. Man, he couldn't remember the last time he'd gotten himself so worked up.

Elise was shaking. Her eyes glistened.

He'd made her cry. Great. Now she'd tell him to go. But she didn't.

"I do care for you, Ryan. I love you. That's why I have to go."

She'd just told him she loved him. She hadn't meant to, even though it was the truth.

Another tear slipped down her cheek. She'd cried far too many of them in the past week. Cried for the dreams she couldn't have. And for the knowledge that the only way to spare his dream of his future home and family was to leave. It had crushed her more than anything she'd ever gone through.

Then she'd walked around the corner to see him

standing there, and the lost look on his face had broken her heart. The desire, the need to fly to him and wrap her arms around him had overwhelmed her. She probably would have done it, too, if not for the heavy box in her arms, reminding her of her resolution.

That box was growing heavier by the second. She shifted it. Ryan moved forward and took it from her. The scent of him made her throat ache. If only...

Setting down the box, he took her hands in his. She tried to pull them back, but he held on. "Elise, darling Elise. I don't understand. If you love me, then why? Don't you know I'm in love with you, too?"

"That's why I have to go."

He gave a half shrug, shaking his head. "That makes absolutely no sense."

Sighing, she dropped her head, allowing herself the brief joy of resting her forehead against his chest. Surely, once she'd explained, he'd see that she was right. He might not like it, but he'd see that a future together would never work.

He was right, though. She'd been wrong to decide she could just leave without explaining. She owed him better than that. Taking a deep breath, she lifted her head and stepped back, ignoring the disappointment on his beloved face.

"Mikey's taking a nap. Let's go in the house so I can explain. I want to leave when he wakes up."

He didn't like that. She could see by the way the frown dug into his face. But he nodded, letting go of her hands. Her instinct was to reach out and grab a hand back. She didn't, though. She needed to sever the connection between them. Squash those impulses. Her sanity depended on it.

Once in the kitchen, she turned down the CD she'd been playing for Mikey. He was having trouble sleeping when it was quiet. Then she sat at the table, waving her hand to the other chair. Instead of taking her hint, he stalked to the counter and leaned against it, arms crossed across his chest.

"How about that explanation? Tell me how you can say you love me and leave."

Ouch. She had really hurt him. That hadn't been her intention, inevitable as it was.

"I told you about my past, but I didn't tell you everything. You know how I told you about my surgery?"

"Honey, what does that have to do with us?"

Lord, help me. This is so hard.

"When my appendix ruptured, followed by the infection, there was internal damage. And it caused scar tissue. A lot of scar tissue. Which means that I can't have kids." She sucked in her breath. "That's the real reason that my fiancé left me. He couldn't accept the fact that I couldn't give him children. It wasn't good for his image. So he found someone who could."

Ryan's face grew somber. She braced herself. "Your fiancé was an idiot. I'm a little offended that you would compare me to him. You can't get pregnant? So what? I knew that was a definite possibility."

Wait—what?

"You knew it was a possibility?" How could he have known and still come after her? Shouldn't he be running in the opposite direction?

He laughed, a short barking laugh without humor. "Elise, I was raised in a family full of doctors, remem-

ber? Surgery issues and scar tissue were normal din-
nertime conversation. Of course I knew."

Pushing back her chair, she stood and began to
pace, rubbing her hands up and down her arms. "It's
more than a possibility, Ryan. It's a fact. I can't have
kids of my own. Not ever." She turned to face him,
holding out a pleading hand. "How could I do that
to you? I know how much you want to be a father. I
listened to you talk to Jackson when we were at the
Bylers' house. I know you want a family. And you'd
be a great father. If I stayed, we'd just grow closer.
And I know you. You'd give up your dream for me. I
couldn't do that to you."

Swallowing past the lump in her throat, she moved
a step closer. "I do love you, but it would kill me to
know that I was the reason you never had the family
you wanted."

Ryan straightened and closed the space between
them. He reached out and placed a warm hand on the
side of her face. "It wouldn't kill my dream if we were
together, Elise. It would just change it a little. And you
do have a child. Mikey may not be your birth child,
but you love him like he was. You don't love him less
because he wasn't born to you, do you?"

"Of course not!" Hope started to take root. Was
it true? Could he really accept this? She couldn't go
through the pain of being rejected again. "It truly
doesn't bother you?"

"Nah. Why should it? I'm adopted myself. All of
my siblings are."

Shock rippled through her, followed by a surge of
joy. "Really?"

Ryan eased his arms around her and pulled her

close. She relaxed against him, feeling the ravages of the past week seep away. God was so good. Why had she doubted Him when He'd brought her this man? For a few minutes, they stood, holding each other.

"Aunty Lise! Mr. Ryan!" Mikey's cry broke them apart seconds before the youngster hurtled into the room and wrapped himself around Ryan's legs. "Mr. Ryan, we going on a trip. I don't wanna go."

Ryan lifted the boy into his strong arms, a smile creasing his face, making his dimples flash into view. Elise caught her breath at the light and love shining in his expression. Not only for her, but for Mikey, too. She was so thankful that he had come after her.

That's when the truth hit her. God had sent her someone who would fight for her. Someone who loved her enough to come after her even after she'd rejected him. *Thank You, Lord.*

"So you'll stay?" Ryan asked her, hope in his eyes.

Laughing softly, she nodded. "In LaMar Pond, yes. But I'm still selling this house. I can't live here. Not after everything that's happened." She looked at Mikey. "What about it, buddy? Think you'd be okay with staying close to Ryan?"

"Yay!" Mikey yelled.

"You said it," Ryan told the little boy, squeezing him tight. "Where are you planning on going?"

"A friend from work said we could stay with her until we find a place. She has lots of room."

Ryan flashed her a tender smile.

"I was thinking this afternoon before I left the station that I wanted to take my two favorite people in the world out to eat. What do you say? I think we have something to celebrate."

She smiled. "I think that sounds like a great idea. What do you say, Mikey?"

Mikey whooped. Laughing, Ryan set the boy on his feet and pulled her close again.

"I'm getting my shoes!" Mikey shouted as he bolted from the room.

Elise started to laugh. Ryan smiled. "While he's doing that…"

He smoothed her hair away from her face and leaned closer. His breath fanned her lips. "Welcome home, Elise."

Her eyes drifted closed as he kissed her.

"Oh, yuck." Laughing, they broke apart to find Mikey scowling in the doorway.

"Let's go eat," Ryan said, chuckling. He grabbed her hand. She gave it a squeeze and offered her other one to Mikey. Happiness swelled inside as she walked outside to go celebrate with her guys.

EPILOGUE

There were people everywhere she looked.

Elise hoped she wouldn't be asked to name the people gathered together at the barbecue. It had been six weeks since she and Ryan had reconciled, and this was her first time to meet the whole family. Apparently, Ryan's parents hosted a barbecue at their place in Grove City every Labor Day weekend. She'd been very nervous when he'd first brought up the idea, inviting her and Mikey to be his guests at the event. She'd accepted apprehensively. In her mind, she had thought family meant parents and siblings.

Little had she known that Ryan's family could fill up a small town on their own. His mother had personally walked her around, introducing her to Ryan's sisters and his brother and their spouses and children. And then there were grandparents. His grandmother had remarried a sweet gentleman who clearly adored her. Then there were the aunts and uncles. Both Ryan's parents had come from large families. Not to mention all the cousins. She'd lost count. Relatives filled the house and spilled over onto the lawn. Everywhere she looked, people were talking, laughing and hugging.

There were worse places to be.

She was shy at first, but Ryan's family seemed to be genuinely interested in her life. As the day progressed, she grew more comfortable.

Mikey had no such problems. The minute Ryan's sister Piper had approached them with her four-year-old daughter in tow, Mikey had let go of his aunt's hand to follow after his new friend.

Elise was gratified to hear his happy squeals of laughter blending in with the rest of the noise. He'd been quiet for too long.

"You okay?" Ryan nudged her shoulder with his arm, gazing down at her with those brown eyes that made her melt every time.

"I'm good. Your family is fantastic."

He looked around, his face relaxed and smiling. The warm glint in his eyes sparked a silent thrill in her spirit. Especially when he looked at her. Then his smile grew tender and eyes deepened, seemed to glow from within. This is what it was to be truly and totally in love. Her hand sought his. She treasured the connection.

"Ryan."

Ryan tensed. Although they'd greeted each other at the door, Ryan had yet to have an actual conversation with his father. Elise knew that theirs was not a comfortable relationship. Ryan's father had been unhappy with the fact that he had gone against his wishes and become a cop. His mother had made strides in coming to grips with his chosen career. But his father? The jury was still out.

Now was the pivotal moment.

The air seemed to be a bit thinner. Ryan's hand

tightened on hers. Then he let go and stepped toward his father. She fought the urge to grab on and pull him back because she knew this conversation had to happen. Or would it be a confrontation? Hopefully not an angry one—not in front of so many people.

"Dad. You look good."

Ryan stood in front of his father. Positioned so close, it was hard to believe they weren't related by blood. Neil Parker was a handsome man, his brown hair—almost the same shade as Ryan's—was salted with silver threads through it. His brown eyes were creased liberally at the edges. That's when she saw it. In his eyes there was a world of grief. And of pride.

He loved his son. His reserve about Ryan's choices hadn't come from disapproval, but because he feared for him. She heard Mikey's high laugh in the background and understood. Parents wanted their children to be safe. But in the end, they also wanted them to be happy.

She relaxed.

"Son." Neil's voice was rusty. He cleared his throat. "Ryan. Your mother and I have done a lot of praying these past few years. About you and for you."

Ryan dipped his head in acknowledgment but didn't say anything. She wasn't sure what he could say to that.

"Especially in the past few weeks. Knowing how much danger you were in. And now, hearing your girlfriend there talking about how you saved her life, and the life of that boy of hers, well, I wanted to let you know… I'm proud of you, son. I don't understand all your choices, but your mother and I have come to realize that they were *your* choices to make.

The last thing I want to do is push you away because I am stubborn."

Blinking, Elise tried to clear the tears blurring her vision. Ryan's jaw was clenched. Not in anger. His throat was working, and his eyes were shiny. He was fighting his own emotional battle. Finally, he gave up and embraced his father. Elise gave up the fight, too, and let her tears fall as she watched her man make peace with his father.

Peace flowed into her. Leaving Ryan to talk with his father, Elise wandered off to see if she could help his mother in the kitchen. Penny and the other women welcomed her warmly. Soon she found herself slicing the freshly baked bread as she chatted with Ryan's family. She'd just finished when a pair of strong arms slipped around her waist.

"Hey, Summer girl. Everything okay with you?"

Turning, Elise put her hands on Ryan's shoulders, grinning at his pet name for her. He'd discovered that her middle name was Summer and decided it fit her.

"Okay, lovebirds. Not in the kitchen. Some people don't want to lose their appetite."

Ryan rolled his eyes at his brother, Chris, but took his arms from around her, only to grab her hand and pull her toward the table. "Fine, fine. Come on, Elise. It's time to eat. You're sitting by me."

As they walked out to the picnic tables so over-flowing with food that the floral tablecloths had disappeared, Elise raised her eyebrows at his sister Rhonda, nodding in her direction with a questioning tilt of her head. Rhonda was madly working with a very fancy camera. One that someone into professional photography would use.

"Oh, don't mind her." Ryan shrugged. "She's obsessed with her camera. Always insists on taking a thousand pics at every gathering. Annoying, but what can you do?"

Rhonda stuck her tongue out at him, but didn't stop.

Elise smiled and followed Ryan to the table.

"Aunt Lise! I'm hungry." Mikey rushed at her. Ryan chuckled.

"Hey, buddy. Just in time for lunch. You can sit here, right next to your aunt." There was a booster chair secured to the bench next to the spot Ryan indicated for her.

Odd. Her napkin was lying on her plate, instead of folded under the silverware like all the rest of them. The kids must have set the table. Amused, she shook her head and pulled off the napkin.

And sucked in her breath.

On her plate, someone had taped a paper heart. In the center were the words *Marry me, please.* Elise could feel all eyes zeroing in on her. Breathless, she turned. Ryan was kneeling on one knee behind her, a stunning solitaire diamond in his hand. Hands flying to her face, she could do nothing to stop the grin that she knew was plastered there. She was vaguely aware of Rhonda snapping pictures rapid-fire. Obviously, she'd been in on the plan.

"Elise, you and Mikey are everything to me. I love you and want to spend my life with you. I want to grow old with you, be a father to Mikey, and if God wills it, maybe adopt some brothers and sisters for him someday. Will you marry me?"

Overcome, she couldn't answer at first. She nodded. Finally, she was able to get out a mangled reply. "Yes."

Ryan rose and placed the ring on her trembling finger. Then he moved to embrace her. Mikey got in the way. "Auntie Lise, does this mean we'll be part of Ryan's family?"

Ryan answered. "It does. That okay with you, little man?"

Mikey pursed his lips for a moment while he considered the man in front of him. Elise started to get nervous. Mikey loved Ryan. She knew he did. She opened her lips, although she had no idea what she planned to say.

After what felt like a lifetime, Mikey grinned. "Awesome sauce."

The watching crowd laughed. Ryan and Elise laughed, too. Ryan leaned forward and kissed his new fiancée.

It was awesome, indeed. She couldn't wait for their life together to begin.

* * * * *

*If you loved this book,
don't miss the other heart-stopping
Amish adventures from Dana R. Lynn's
Amish Country Justice series:*

Plain Target
Plain Retribution
Amish Christmas Abduction

Find more great reads at www.LoveInspired.com.

Dear Reader,

I had no idea when I wrote my first book how much I would grow to love LaMar Pond and the people who live there. Through the past few years, though, it has become so much more than a fictional town to me. I have enjoyed "visiting" the small Pennsylvania town and telling the stories of the characters as they find their happy-ever-afters. *Amish Country Ambush* was no different.

We first met Ryan Parker in *Plain Retribution*. He's got a heart of gold and a bit of a chip on his shoulder. He doesn't realize it, but he has so much to offer a woman. A woman like Elise St. Clair. Elise is not well-known in LaMar Pond. She has suffered so much in her life and struggles to realize that she is worthy to be loved. She also has a stubborn streak. These two were so much fun to write about as they grew closer and learned how to open up and let love in while racing against the clock. I hope you enjoyed their story.

Thank you for joining me for Ryan and Elise's story. I love to hear from readers. You can email me at WriterDanaLynn@gmail.com. Or visit me online at www.danarlynn.com. I am also on Facebook and Twitter (@danarlynn).

Blessings,

Dana R. Lynn

Get 4 **FREE REWARDS!**

We'll send you 2 FREE Books <u>plus</u> 2 FREE Mystery Gifts.

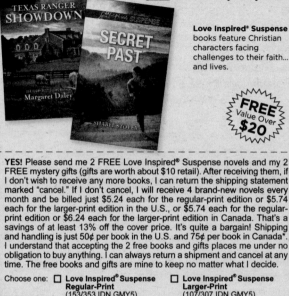

Love Inspired® Suspense books feature Christian characters facing challenges to their faith... and lives.

FREE Value Over **$20**

SPECIAL EXCERPT FROM

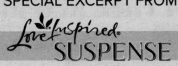
Love Inspired.
SUSPENSE

*A reporter enlists the help of a soldier and his
bomb-sniffing dog to stay one step ahead of the
bomber who wants her dead.*

Read on for a sneak preview of
Explosive Force *by Lynette Eason,*
the next book in the Military K-9 Unit miniseries,
available September 2018 from Love Inspired Suspense.

First Lieutenant Heidi Jenks, news reporter for CAF News,
blew a lock of hair out of her eyes and did her best to keep
from muttering under her breath about the boring stories
she was being assigned lately.

Heidi shut the door to the church where her interviewee
had insisted on meeting and walked down the steps. She
shivered and glanced over her shoulder. For some reason
she expected to see Boyd Sullivan, as if the fact that she
was alone in the dark would automatically mean the serial
killer was behind her.

After being chased by law enforcement last week, he'd
fallen from a bluff and was thought to be dead. But when
his body was never found, that assumption changed. He
was alive. Somewhere.

Heidi's steps took her past the base hospital. She was
getting ready to turn onto the street that would take her

home when a flash of movement from the K-9 training center caught her eye. Her steps slowed, and she heard a door slam.

A figure wearing a dark hoodie bolted down the steps and shot off toward the woods behind the center. He reached up, shoved the hoodie away and yanked something—a ski mask?—off his head then pulled the hoodie back up. He stuffed the ski mask into his jacket pocket.

Very weird actions that set Heidi's internal alarm bells screaming. She decided it was prudent to get out of sight.

Just as she moved to do so, the man spun.

And came to an abrupt halt as his eyes locked on hers.

Ice invaded her veins. He took a step toward her then shot a look back at the training center. With one last threatening glare, he whirled and raced toward the woods once again.

Like he wanted to put as much distance between him and the building as possible.

Don't miss
Explosive Force *by Lynette Eason,*
available September 2018 wherever
Love Inspired® Suspense books and ebooks are sold.

www.LoveInspired.com

LISEXP0818

Looking for inspiration in tales
of hope, faith and heartfelt romance?

Check out **Love Inspired**® and
Love Inspired® **Suspense** books!

New books available every month!

CONNECT WITH US AT:

Harlequin.com/Community

Facebook.com/HarlequinBooks

Twitter.com/HarlequinBooks

Instagram.com/HarlequinBooks

Pinterest.com/HarlequinBooks

ReaderService.com

Love Inspired®

LIGENRE2018